SEX AND THE SINGLE CAMEL

SEX
AND THE
SINGLE CAMEL

A Novel by

PHIL CLENDENEN

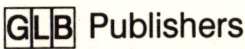 Publishers   San Francisco

Published in the United States by
GLB Publishers
P.O. Box 78212, San Francisco, CA 94107 USA

Cover by Curium Design
Cover photography by Ken Perez

Publisher's Cataloging in Publication
(Prepared by Quality Books Inc.)

Clendenen, Phil.
    Sex and the single camel / by Phil Clendenen.
    p. cm.
    ISBN 1-879194-18-X

    1. Gay men--Morocco--Tangier--Fiction. 2. Tangier (Morocco)--Fiction. I. Title.

PS3553.L453S4 1994   813'.54
                                        QBI94-930

First printing, September, 1994
10 9 8 7 6 5 4 3 2 1

**For my family.
And C-Span.**

I want to thank Bill Warner of GLB Publishers
for his expert editing and advice, plus his patience.

The desire for perfection may be the worst disease that ever afflicted the human mind.

— Louis de Fontanes, to Napoleon

SEX AND THE SINGLE CAMEL

CHAPTERS

KHALID, TV* SERVICE PERSON

Night and my knees hurt. Two wanders today down to Tanger Bay near the train station for cheaper, more delicious food where the real Moroccans seemed to be eating.

Then miles through the ancient Medina, mazes of paved footpaths between pastel mud tenements nearly meeting overhead, leaning on each other for centuries. Some Moroccan men and women wearing jellabas (hooded robes), just like a Cecil B. DeMille tits-and-sandals Biblical epic fantasy!

But the low flat part of the Medina's alley-streets was mostly tiny tourist shops, bulging with tasty inexpensive everythings and friendly Spanish-speaking merchants. "Only look, no buy!" they all knew in English, and I did, to learn the new territory and sharpen my bargaining tongue, for if the job came through, I'd be living here. Yes! Tanger ("TaanHAIR"), a friendly Arab city where most people kinda spoke Spanish. A San Francisco Mission District blond Chicano from Kansas' dream come true!

Then steep hills back to my hotel – Tanger ups and downs like San Francisco. But smaller for walking everywhere, with no buses, just collective taxis, Mercedes, Fiats and Renaults. Yes, I could live here– and the men!

"Hi Englishman! Welcome to Tanger, I you friend new Khalid!" coming up fast on my right ear in the night crowd on main drag Boulevard Pasteur.

"¿Cómo estás pues, qué onda ese?" I replied. It was

---

* "Watching TV" was old hippie code for smoking pot, back in the days when the possession of a joint, or even a roach, could land you in the pokey. It is preserved here as code for smoking hash.

1

easier to use my Mexican/Mission District Spanish here because few Tangerinos ("Taan-hair-REE-nos") seemed to speak conversational English. So most of them assumed I was from Spain across the Straits of Gibraltar, which made things easier. For when I was brash enough on my first day here to volunteer I was Californiano, the Moroccans fawned all over me, arms around patting and all smiling teeth, "Ah Americano! Welcome to Morocco amigo bueno, bueno!"

Being an anonymous hero got tiresome right quick. But the lonely Moroccans missed their buenos Americanos dólares touristos since the Gulf War. What a joke; Morocco was as much Iraq as my hometown, Saliva, Kansas, was the South Bronx. Some Moroccan men even wore black USA caps with golden cluster leaves on the brims.

And now I'm watching TV. The easy listening channel glided me through jerky hotel room logistics; I'm looking forward to my coffin where everything can be reached from the bed. My trusty Sony portable on Radio Naccional with a French-speaking deejay playing American, British, Spanish, French and Arab rock n roll and everything else. Yes! A delicious nutz n honey mix, just like Don't Call It Frisco, unless you sometimes live there.

Peeling sticky clothes, soft Moroccan giggle TV, oh! hot blast tingle showershower clothes-wash. Sometime later found me in air–armchair, only tiny TV glowing in the dark, with a liter of Eau minerale Sidi Ali in one hand and una cerveza Speciale Flag Brassieries du Maroc in the other. Cold bay whispers through wide double windows, first night Tangerino zenning pale shadowed wall on the other side of hotel airshaft, for an eon.

Ingratiating Khalid and I simple Spanish-chat along Boulevard Pasteur. It was blocked off on summer nights for pedestrians, mostly Arab tourists, lots of Moroccans here for cooler convergence of ocean and bay and August on the beach.

Khalid's español, his third language after Arabic and French, was seriously deficient but with strong body language, his arm around pulling me, "Now we go to friend's beautiful shop, only look no buy, your friend Khalid get you native Tangerino price, Por Dios!"

Laughing español, "Fuck no, Khalid my dear friend, I'll just sit out here and you go in, look no buy native Americano price."

Laugh-slapping my hand, Khalid went into the shop. My knees were killing me so I sat on a small camel bench outside, appreciating quality weavings, leather, wood, fabrics, metal and ceramics on display outside and in the window.

Le Boulevard Pasteur seemed so sidewalk cafe European, with dark-skinned people, like a together Mexico – clean, odorless restrooms in even the $3 – 4 entree restaurants today. But BYOP (bring your own paper).

Charming young Khalid danced out of the shop and his appearance surprised me again: scabbed cut on his forehead, several discolored teeth missing, poor clothes, unshaven. But he was the first one to come up to me as I was babystepping down the crowded Boulevard to save my knees while looking open and making eye contact, an over-time sport here if you want. Was it curiosity, or sex, or both? Oh, por favor goddesses!

I cursed my aching knees in dirty Mexicano to clucking, sympathetic Khalid, and pled to be guided to Los Baños Turqueños, where, my taxi driver from the Spain ferry assured me today, they had saunas, jacuzzis and eager young men who did everything. The bees knees, with Trojanez and KY in my counterfeit Benetton shorts, $3.50 from the Patunam Market in Bangkok, which always turned the washwater a natty pale blue.

Skinny but strong arms pulled tourist in distress up off the camel bench. Cooing Khalid led me up a dimly lit side

3

street to a dark, unmarked metal door. He banged on it, no answer.

"Se cirrido!" ("Closed!" in lousy Spanish), dramatic Khalid excessively gestured. He was either very dumb or had been speed reading his TV Guide or something. But quick enough to swoop me up the narrow street, confiding loudly in his fractured español, "No problem, I know where we can go! Your oldest amigo Tangerino Khalid take care of you, take you to best hamman (baths in Arabic) very near. Honest Khalid save your dollar with price Tangerino!"

Yeah. But my durable Walgreen's flipflops accompanied the garrulous guide up and down dim streets that at least had occasional cars on them. But then he snaked me through narrow tunnels of dusty tenements where the real Moroccans lived; I was slightly paranoid. Silent men, women all in jellabas, some scarved or veiled. And lots of kids playing on the two meter wide walkways – all studying me on their turf – not the easy anonymity of Tourist Pasteur and the Bayfront.

Ah, but I had mouthy Khalid to protect me; he had a wife, two kids, spoke six languages, called me his dearest friend. Shuttling me quickly through the poor district, he wasn't obnoxious butch macho, more laughy pushy asshole.

At last down an empty alley street to los baños turqueños with a shabby sign, "Hamman" and written in Arabic too; and a lighted doorway Khalid gently shoved me through.

I fumbled out the 7 dirham (80¢) admission fee at the old counter to an older man speaking fast Arabic with Khalid who pulled me inside. Hey, this wasn't the deal! We had agreed on $1 for guide to the baths and that was it; except it is never it.

The bath's large entrance included a worn but clean locker room with benches where I stripped to my sturdy Hanes, assisted by serious Khalid while watching several

4

handsome Moroccans doing same, theirs white cotton briefs with attractive soft bulges.

But this joint smelled straight; didn't these damn guides ever get anything right? Where was my infamous storied Tanger of Barbary Pirates, smuggling and natural bisexuality? Khalid removed only his worn sandals to tour underweared me through the baths, an aged attendant locking my clothes in a wooden locker.

Inside my first baños Tangerinos — a tiled, cubicled washing room and a warm wet sauna — that was all. Moroccan men in their underwear washed themselves or each other in open cubicles, while in the sauna, most slumped gossiping, a few stretching arms and legs in pairs. The only overt signs of affection were their Arabic voices, sweet music I didn't know the words to.

"Now I wash you!" enthused gay(?) Khalid. "Each pail of water only 1 dirham (11¢). I get you price Tangerino, no tourist price for my dearest friend!" his beautiful black eyes wide, feigning perfect sincerity.

Khalid tossed off his red shirt, his chest hairless and scrawny-hard with flat black nips, still wearing his dark pants. Goddesses, should I invite him in for a swim? But I didn't even like my new dearest friend that much. And his green missing teeth – well, I knew it was imperialist thinking, but hardongs are rarely politically correct.

Laughing Khalid fetching in plastic pails, splashing warm, hot, then ouchy cold water over me in our open cubicle, pleasure so overwhelming I ignored our few fellow-washers watching us from the neutrality of their own cubicles. At least they weren't running over to clap my tender back, shouting, "Welcome to Morocco, Americano Muy Bueno Amigo!"

Khalid's energetic hand in an abrasive mitt with a bar of soap inside scrubbed me then shampooed me all over. He squat-jumped back laughing when his soapy bare hand touched the angry red head escaping the elastic of my

5

sopping Hanes.

Maybe had I paid friendly Khalid's 80¢ admission fee, we would have washed each other and be mutually whacking off crazily but surreptitiously under our slick underwear. But my wheels turn more slowly in foreign cultures; I was confused when he barged in with me, plus where was the beautiful-young-men-doing-everything room?

My knees pressing worn white-tiled warm sauna wall, no pain though we'd walked a piece. A lookee no touchee prickee teasee place, smiling eyes and hellos, but friendly hunks' humps cut off by untouched white cotton briefs. Not even nudie shower play like in the frat house back at K.U.

Bored, so vamos pues. Sitting on the bench in the old locker room, sober Khalid with his shirt back on towelled me off around my dripping underwear, my frustrated bone gone — wouldn't want his wife two kids to lose face in my Hanes.

Khalid tenderly feeling my forehead, in concerned español, "Oh my best friend, you must sit here long time here with your dearest friend Khalid Por Dios until your delicate body so Americano accustoms itself to cold night Tangerino air!" shivering vigorously.

Yeah. For a San Franciscan, it was a heat wave out there, no fog nor gale winds. After shouting Arabic orders at the aged counterman, expressive Khalid rubbed his shapely brown neck painfully. "The cool juice of the orange is very necessary to cleanse and purify our bodies and minds after our refreshing baths."

Fuck metaphysics, I was craning my honky neck trying to scope out the juice squeezer behind the antique counter. Thank god I couldn't see it, only a picture of King Hassan II in a fez above the counter; maybe he'd keep an eye on the kitchen sanitation for me.

Delicious fresh squeezed of course, and Khalid taught

me to toast in Arabic, "Sáha!" And there were only one, two, three teeth missing, but in front, fights? And they weren't really green, more an interesting stained marbled rust color.

Scrubs sprawled on the bench in the old locker room, Khalid bragging he was a TV service person, a safe job he assured me, his most trustworthy friend. Shrugging sadly his wife two kids needing milk, he pressed me for a service call tonight. Laughing, I agreed, but tomorrow, for here was deep in his territory.

Back and forth bull, I wasn't catching it all because breathless Khalid was fast-dropping French into his garbage Spanish, with a little underdeveloped English on the side. He claimed to speak six languages perfectly – he probably did – in una ensalada mixta.

Gracious host Khalid got the bill on a scrap of gray wrapping paper, itemized in hand-printed French, which I could figure out (one year, D's at Saliva High). But pushy Khalid insisted on overexplaining: 59 dirham – each water bucket became 2 dirham for Bueno Amigo Americano, 4 dirham for the rough washmitt now hanging in my shower, and shampoo, rented locker, towel, and plastic scraper great for bottoms of hooves, plus tip. $6+ for friendly homeboy baths, no fuckee but no knee pain, gracias obnoxious guide Khalid.

Grabbing one of my remaining Carlton 100's, Khalid performed meticulous television surgery on it, and clicked on the old TV right there in front of ancient attendants and several dark temptations undressing down to their briefs, as we slowly became remote controlled.

But I spied on them all watching me – why did my first Tangerino TV show have to be Paranoid Home Videos?

"This is my city, I Tangerino!" scoffed proud Khalid. "And my fathers too, they all know me here, they don't care. And your Khalid protect you – protect most innocent Californiano from every other thieving puto (male whore) on Le Boulevard!"

"Gracias, but no gracias, papá." We laughed and really rapped baby, casual Khalid's hairless short-fingered hand on my bare underweared thigh. Confidentially, "You know, Tanger is the center of the whole world!"

Laugh-slapping his back sharply, "Sure ese, cuz we're here, Khalid my silliest motherfucker!"

Indignant scabs pulsing his brown forehead, "No no, you don't believe me? Hah! Just study satellite photographs of the Earth and you'll see Por Dios, Tanger always right in the middle, hah!"

Nodding gravely, "I appreciate our little-science discussion, my most scholarly hamman companion."

Khalid humorously pushy, but then so am I at work, "OK, then you go with me right now tonight, you need more this good educational TV Por Dios!"

OK, I laugh-dressed myself and we left amid thanks, blessings in Arabic and French. Lighter than air hit dark, chill-breathing street in wet underwear under Benettons, yes! Zigzagging up and down sometimes lit, littered walkways with a few silent jellaba'ed people, my antennae gently bristling, zoned in strangelandia, a long way from Louis Pasteur.

Down dusky step street, quiet Khalid sat me on a ceramic doorstep, then spoke past two young men in the shadowed passageway of a house below. Earlier, helpful Khalid had suggested giving him the dinero and meeting later in a cafe on safe Pasteur — ha, no can do.

So sitting on my shadowed step, breathe-remembering a TV call in the slums of TJ, the ominous talking cop, then a bloodied man carried out of a shack near the border; I was with that butch number from Huanahuato who loved to be fucked — you can never figure.

Khalid back quick, handed me a lump in saranwrap, deep into my pocket, no mention of dinero. In our two previous price discussions, perhaps 17 dirham per (2 bucks) mentioned first, second was all vagueness and fog but I ordered the five channel special. Oh well, I'd learned to be an emotional bargainer.

"Muchísimas gracias Khalid ese, amigazo. Now I'd like to return to my humble hotel room to write in my secret travel TV journal," always the perfect excuse.

Anguish grabbing my arm on deserted, dim street, tragic scabbed face in mine, yuk cigarette breath. "Oh no no! My only friend in my lonesome life Por Dios, now we go to a little park only I know, to try out TV so you will know Honest Khalid not cheat you — no no, not like those thieving putos on Le Boulevard — I protect you!" clinging to me.

Reassuring back pats unclinging him, "It's cool Khalid, I trust you." Hah! "And thank you so much for your kind invitation to the deserted park. But it's my first day here and I'm a little tired, though my knees don't hurt anymore, gracias pues."

Khalid beaming, "I cure you, now Khalid your only doctor, help you for life Por Dios!" tender kissing my surprised forehead. We walked on, hand in hand sweet Arab style — just like Castro Street without the psychotic teenagers with baseball bats. Taking advantage of the tender mood, "So how much do I owe you, Khalid, my latest friend?"

Angelfood choirboy's black sinner eyes pleading to Allah in a dusty street light, "Oh you know you mean more to me than my very own mother, whatever you so generously offer poor Khalid, he gratefully and humbly accept Por Dios!"

Angry Khalid upped me three times to 200 dirham ($22) for wife two kids' milk, hamman scrub included. We walked the long way home above Tanger Bay's twinkling lights, refrigerator winds drying our sweat instantly, another peninsula bay city, yes!

"Now we go to bar, I pay the everything!" my new

9

friend dragging me off again.

Fullstop: "Gee thanks so much my oldest friend Khalid, but *now* I go home *now* and write in many colored channels *now*."

Laughing gentle shovings, "Then we meet tomorrow, everyday, your hotel 5 p.m."

"Thanks so much, my most faithful companion, but this is my vacation and I don't want no fuckin' plans," except finding the real goddamn baños turqueños mañana!

Holding me sincerely, shiny dark eyes glittering up at mine, new lover's voice, "I be outside at cafe by your hotel tomorrow, everyday 5 p.m."

He didn't even know hotel's goddamn name, but there would surely be a sidewalk cafe nearby. Swaggering Khalid accompanied his latest hostage Americano to a liquor store (many Moroccans are Jack Muslims), where I ordered one beer-to-go for each of us – shedding time. Khalid, shocked, said I surely meant ten apiece.

"No, one," I smiled.

Khalid's superior laugh, "Por Dios one isn't worth it unless you have two!" but capitulated and accepted one when my vacant smile tugged the center of his universe back to puto Tanger.

He walked me quietly to my hotel no visitors allowed chaio pues.

10

RENAULT LUST

Sidewalk cafe sitting, the national sport – watching late afternoon life as sweet as scalding glasses of Moroccan tea seeping mint stalk and leaves. I probed Khalid for tourist lore, history not his strong suit, across a petite awning-shaded table where he was waiting for me at 5 p.m. as promised.

En español confidencial, "What I really meant last night, Khalid, was that I wanted a guide to los baños turqueños with fucky-fucky men, not just to take a fuckin' bath, if you know what I mean. Though thank you very much, and the TV miracle healer cured my aching knees."

Smiling Khalid had cleaned up. Freshly shaven, scabs disappeared leaving thin pink lines on his handsome cafe au lait face, short black sheeps-wool hair wet, pressed pale lemon shirt. But he couldn't wash off nor slick back the ingratiating fellowrat in him.

Rusty gapped smile, "That can be easily arranged. You want to go there and do that thing with me, you and I together? I know where we can go!"

Leaning back grin, "Sure, why not?" For maybe Khalid as fuckbuddy would help me get over Kansaño middle-class hang ups, like good teeth and rational conversation.

Khalid forward, softly, "I never did that thing, with another man before."

My laughter spit hot tea, "That's a fucking lie!"

For bluntness is a way to break through hustlers' sentimental cliches; strength and cunning they understand and respect.

Khalid's street growl, "¡La Palabra Es La Palabra! (The Word Is The Word!) You must respect the word of True Friend Khalid, I never lie, only when absolutely necessary Por Dios!"

"Sí pues. So how much are these real fucky-fucky baths

11

gonna cost us?"

"Shhh! You disgrace your best friend!" Deal time, dark eyes locked on: "Oh very expensive to do that thing en los baños, forty-fifty dollar."

"Horseshit ese! I'll pay 100 dirham ($11) not one cent more! At my hotel I asked them what the minimum wage was here; they said it's 5 dirham per hour, that's 40 dirham a day. And I'm more than doubling that for a few hours, or if you're lucky an all-nighter, of easy acting, cuz I'm hot! Such a deal, Khalid baby!"

Laughing weary patience, Khalid lit another black market Marlboro and sipped his tea. How did they make one glass last so long, I was already on my second!

Excited head in, low, "I know where we can go for free Por Dios! An abandoned house in my neighborhood very near, there's an old car in the garage, very comfortable for us to do that thing in."

Deal closing snakesmile that forgot to brush, "And it will cost you absolutely nothing, my newest wife!"

Yeah. There will probably be kids guarding the car, extorting tips. "Isn't that a little dangerous Khalid, my newest wife — what about the police?"

"I Tangerino man! I know all the police, they all know my father — they say we have the same face," framing a pathetic angel smile attempt with his hands, his tooth gaps actually kinda erotic if you didn't think about them.

Khalid grabbing my bare knee under the table, "You want to watch TV with police? I know where they go Por Dios!"

My knee squirming away from nutty hand, "Oh thank you but no thank you very much, I think rocking the abandoned car will be enough for tonight. "¿Nos vamos pues?"

Smile of ancient wisdom and hand of restraint on my thigh, "Finish our tea, rest, we have much time, wait for the sun to sleep, my too-eager friend."

12

Sigh, "Yeah, smaller sips, slower steps, this is my vacation — lasting longer than I'd intended. The company director got called to Nueva York for some silly emergency and no job interview until he gets back in two weeks. So now I'm a careful Californiano playboy watching my dirham."

Grimacing, mournfully, "Oh money fills the life with pain and tears. Por Dios I need 500 dirham a day for my poor life, and I live with my father and brothers."

Hah! What happened to wife two kids' milk money of last night's TV fee debate? But why catch a friend's harmless bargaining lie when the whoppers were running?

"You're so lucky you're rich, Khalid. I'm living on less than 300 dirham a day, 30 lousy bucks and about a third of that is for my too-nice hotel."

Defensive thigh grip, "Oh no you rich, poor Khalid very poor Por Dios! Jobs difficult in Marhuecos (Morocco). Marhuecos has much food but not job." Relaxing, "But I have my health, yes, Peace and Health, The Most Blessed Gifts of the Life, blah, blah, blah."

Nodding and uh-huhing, I switched channels to Boulevard Pasteur's promenade of mostly Arab tourists in casual, smart Western dress, but only Europeans in shorts, damnit. Sweet mint tea, idle laughing bullshit, bay breeze picking up. I paid, Khalid picked up and pocketed the 2 dirham tip, explaining it wasn't the custom here. I didn't cause a fuss, but I always tipped when there was no service charge on the bill — imagine a waiters' hourly pay here!

Up shaded twisting streets — actually we walked mostly in the streets, along the parked cars, because the sidewalks were so narrow and crowded. Streets were one-lane and one-way, the slow traffic and pedestrians merging smoothly with few honks; people holding conversations standing way out in the street, even in Saliva KS they'd be deadmeat in seconds.

Khalid looking down, shielding his face with his hand

13

from oncoming pedestrians, though foot traffic was light as we entered a neighborhood of imposing high-walled homes, purple and blue flowers tumbling. Khalid a rich kid gone awry?

Low, "I don't want neighbors to make a scandal. They think I do bad thing with foreigner Por Dios!"

Chortle-shoving him, "You are doing bad things to your pobre innocente Californiano!"

Grabbing my bicep too hard, "Shhh! Talk English Por Dios most of them understand Spanish!"

We continued silently as night settled, down a short cul-du-sac, squeezing through a rusty gate to minimize its squeak. Across a small lawn piled with ruins of a gutted house, then into the pitch black skeletal house by cigarette lighter, brave flipflops gripping mounds of debris. Smells of dogshit, yuk, but hand on Khalid's arm followed his lighter.

In an attached garage sat a small car, mostly covered with piles of thin dry branches, faggot kindling camouflage? We struggled into the car by lighter — the smell inside was more of sweet musty abandoned chicken house, downright nostalgic pleasant after the dogshit.

The car's instrument panel and radio had been looted, but its seats were comfy and clean; helpful chauffeur Khalid reclined them both flat. We lay there, smoking, sweating, eyes widening to the shadowed sticks piled against car windows, listening to kids' cries in their own street games on the other side of the flimsy garage door. It didn't even seem weird, had I gone round the bend? In fact, with a couple of TV trays you could fix this place up real nice.

Face to face, lying in the near dark, hushed español, "How much you pay me for doing this?"

Hushed bravado, "How much does your bumbling inexperienced incompetence demand?"

"Oh no no!" blowing a Marlboro cloud in my face, I

retaliating. "You offer to me first Por Dios, is polite. Real Man put others in front of him."

In front of a firing squad maybe. Touching his face, smooth, nice stubble, "My dearest virgin sperm, you should pay me for first most important lesson from experienced compassionate teacher."

Low giggling hand rubbing hairs on my bare thigh, "You funny man, you tell me how much you pay poor Khalid so frightened of your giant red Americano camel Por Dios!"

He resisted my pushing his fingers to shake hands with my camel. "Khalid ese, I'm poor no job, you're rich two jobs."

His thigh hand too tight, "What two jobs I have?"

"Ah my busy Khalid, you're a tourist guide and a TV guide. And after tonight, you can have three jobs!"

Relaxed hushed giggles, fingers tingling under shorts, camel raising Hanes, "I love you more than my own mother Por Dios, how much you pay me now?"

Courage in near darkness, "One hundred dirham and not one fucking peso more!"

Aghast fingers out counting seriously, "¡Por Dios! After I do this thing with you, like my own brother, I must go to los baños to wash myself many times, especially the important parts. Sixty dirham for the baths and nothing for poor violated Khalid lose his manhood to take-advantage foreigner? No no, it is a dangerous thing I do, might get sick, go to doctor, hospital very expensive in Marhuecos Por Dios!"

Dark mutterings, "Oh shut the fuck up, Tallulah Bankhead! I practice safe sex, have you ever heard of condoms?"

"Of course, I don't like. I must have 200 dirham."

"No fuckin' way Khalid Jose, that's more than twice the price of my hotel room, and it even has a hot shower! 125 dirham, that's it, finito!"

15

Khalid mopped his face again with his purple bandana handkerchief ("from America!"), then wiped mine. Sighing, "It is too hot here, let us do this thing now."

He struggled out of his Levi's and swimsuit underwear, I did the same with baggy blue Benetton shorts and Hanes, checking buttoned wallet pocket and my 300 dirham neat in bottom of side pocket. Then Benettons folded and stuck between side of seat and door near my head. It's such a bother sometimes being the rich Americano.

Shirts off, rubbing began. Tonguing hard button tits and baby belly button, thick curly pubes between my teeth, short stubby cock kissed down my throat, my wet fuck finger plying his hairy hairy asshole groaning.

Complimenting my camel's girth, he jacked it, I slowed him, adding saliva and mutual moans. He timidly kissed rearing camel, and tasted its thundering humps.

Fast food sex, wet dream stuff − the lust of bartering had been more personal. But rocks is rocks and getting them off high therapy. Sweaty and dry-mouthed, I rolled away to my respective seat and we jerked on our ownselves for awhile − Khalid using short tight strokes near his chorizo's head − interesting how people in different cultures beat their meat.

Rolling back together face to face, not kissing, banging legs under the dashboard, we wadshot mostly on each other, not in the holiest of holes. Sweaty panting, falling apart, hearts audible in our car of dark sticks, occasional cries of children's street play, each lying in his own seat separate.

"Whew, that was pretty good for a virgin. After a lot more practice in different locations, you'll be able to charge for this someday, Khalid my newest fuckbuddy."

Mutter, "Give me my 200 dirham now Por Dios."

Sensibly, "It's too dark in here, wait till we get outside."

After handkerchief wipings by giggling lighter light, we pulled up trow and returned our seats to their original upright positions, so no one would know, whispered Khalid. We manuevered by lighter through the sticks and across rubbish in the house. Khalid peered out the gate, motioned me onto the street, he hiding his face, I savoring the pungent odor of his leche, milk, as he called it, on my wispy blond moustache and fingers, dessert, as we swiftly left the neighborhood.

"Walk faster!" he hissed back at me, single-file playing spy on the shadowed side of dimstreet in Badass Old Tanger at last.

Back downtown, Khalid led me into a hole-in-the-wall standup dairy bar. He enthusiastically introduced me in Arabic as his wife(?) to two friends who ran the place, and to leven, similar to buttermilk. But better, insisted Khalid, because leven was completely natural, not made in factory like everything in America; precisely what I was worried about. Plus the water still dripping off the glasses pulled from under the counter for the leven, Tangerino Civilization not yet having reached the Disposable Styrofoam Age. The leven was tasty and the price right, 35¢ for two, only 40¢ for a liter to go, urged Khalid. A ver− (we'll see−)

On the downtown streets, old men in woolen jellabas with shiny brass badges guarded parked cars along the curb, collecting 1 dirham tips (11¢) from the drivers. Some of them wore red or white high-top tennies under their jellabas, with sticks to guard Mercedes and Peugeots instead of sheep and goats.

On a side street near my hotel, I handed Khalid 150 dirham and our sotto-voiced battle began, under a red plastic six-shooter sticking out into the street blinking RANCHO DISCO.

No more dearest friend: "No no! You promised me 200 dirham for disgracing my manhood Por Dios and La Palabra Es La Palabra, for friends one to another and for the world entire!" Soft touching, "But no no, you not friend, you more like my wife to me. Last night I cure you

17

in my hamman and set up your TV, and tonight, well, I do more, much much more, than any thieving puto (male whore) Tangerino tourist guide ever do before, my virgin wife Por Dios!" quick embrace and lip kiss.

In-face time, but cool, "Bullfuckingshit dude! I said 125 and gave you 150 and we didn't hardly do anything, it wasn't even worth that!"

Insulted pout, thrusting money at me, "Take it back, take it all back Por Dios my most satan-tongued wife!"

Arm around, soft, "No Khalid, my most tempetuous wife," (he stiffened, "No!"), "you keep the 150 and I'll keep the 50 for a new chapeau, or a dish lunch with the girls."

Ditto soft arm and voice, "No no you give me the 50 dirham to wash myself of our beautiful pollution, my only wife," lip brush with flick of Tangerino tongue. Quick learner for a virgin.

After a brief struggle for face, I surrendered, too embarrassed to yell on the quiet street for mild-mannered Kansaño. Indignant, low, "This is the last time we ever fuck, Khalid, ¡nunca jamás! And if any handsome man comes up to me on Le Boulevard and says anything more than 100 dirham, then it's chaio motherfucker, and that means you, my most grasping ex-wife!"

Concern gripping my arm, "Then you not come to my home tomorrow night, meet my father and brothers?" (Did mothers exist here?) "We give you real meal," (Ah, there she was!), "real meal Marhueco. Give you fine leather belt from my father's shop, very famous is the leather Marhueco."

Sarcasm cuffing ducking head, "You mean you take rich Americano wife home to get family dowry after brief honeymoon en coche? Muchas gracias but fuck you very much, I want many husbands Tangerinos."

Furrowed brow, "Ah but that cannot be, no no."

"Don't you have many women, Khalid?"

Cloud clearing smile, "But yes Por Dios!"

18

Flip— "Then I can fuck your ancient father tomorrow night – en la coche abandonada?"

Shocked laughter pushing me, "Por Dios you too crazy, I think I not want you for wife."

"Hah! And listen, Ms. Khalid, you must now get a real job, maybe two, to support me in luxury, the Holiest of Gifts – "

Razzing goodbyes, kissing cheeks French-style — I meet my new Moroccan family tomorrow night for the most blessed gift of friendly anthropology, not dirham sexology which has thrust me deeply into that unholiest of holes, high rolling low.

AT HOME

From his worn 501's pocket, Khalid slipped out a tan petrified baby turd in plastic wrap. He unwrapped and laid it on the cafe table between us, touched his lighter flame to it, then instructed me en español to scrape off gooey pieces with my thumbnail and roll them into little balls to prepare our 5 p.m. TV dinner zigzagged with Marlboro.

It brightened the reception from our cafe balcony of Moroccan men below in Western dress, sipping cafe o té on miniature shimmering white tabletops, and watching an interminable long distance running event in the Japan International Games on the large screen TV with Arabic voiceover hanging in the lazy afternoon cafe.

Blue tile danced on white walls with the ubiquitous framed, glassed photograph of King Hassan II in a suit, this one the smiley businessman welcoming investment. With the Moroccan flag in the background, simple deep red with a green five-pointed star, so Christmasy.

Dark wood trim and coffee bar, back stairs up to a half-balcony with several tables for two, where we sat, in the special smoking section with beclouded TV fans wafting away the hot August Tangerino hours — it must be 90°, killer heat for Frisco boy.

It was gabby Khalid's place. "Some days I make my TV service rounds down at the dock for the ferries from España, y en las plazas de turistas, but other days, like today hah, I feel like not working at all."

Back to scruffy today, Khalid's dull clothes exhuded slight B.O., rare here. He bogarted, the local custom, "Many my relative arrive from Asilah, sleep in my house, too much people Por Dios!"

A negation of last night's heartfelt in-vite for din-meet-fam? And what about my fine Marhueco belt dowry?

20

Was he weaseling on taking his foreign trick to rich family – or no house and fam – or was he even possibly telling the truth?

Breaking my fixation with street scenes below through wall-to-wall windows we were sitting next to for view and a modicum of breeze, I grabbed the TV; sweetly, "Oh, so what did you do today, my busy Khalid?"

He remembered to taste his cafe au lait, "Oh, I didn't do anything, go out, watch TV with my friends, too much relative in my house."

I heard it the first time, fuckface. Needle, "So why don't you work in your father's tourist shop, Khalid?"

Disgusted, "Too boring – sit for two, three hour Por Dios!"

"Just like the cafes – and lots of tourists go by for you to practice your many languages on."

We were in our usual simple español, his English even worse than my nearly non-existent French, the universal second language studied in all the schools here, Morocco a French colony until 1956. Using Arabic was out of the question at this early point in my Tangerino career. Khalid's favorite Spanish verb form was the past participle with tense to be guessed at. He also said "ayeri" for ayer (yesterday) – he even looked Italian, a small-timer on the wharves of Napoli. Schools too boring, he proclaimed, languages, everything best learned on the streets.

Back to bogart, "No I don't like shop, too boring."

"Like last night."

Liquid black eyes splashed, "Not boring! Por Dios la coche se muy bonito!"

Worm turning screw, "Did you brag to your family yet about getting your macho cherry busted by the finger of educated foreigner in the ancient Renault?"

Drawing back, puzzled, "Why I tell them such a thing?"

Cynical chuckle, "Lighten up, Jack, it's natural. Plenty dudes here do that thang they say."

21

Disapproving, "Shhh! Not true!"

"You mean more talk than do? Just like humans – "

Khalid smiled neutrally – never sure how much he, I understood, for no subtitles on our little tragi-comedy, so had to rely more on acting and cultural nuance.

Actually, through the balcony picture windows, I was watching four teenage black market Marlboro men playing in traffic in the intersection below, a four-way stop with captive clients. With several packs in hand and more up loose jacket sleeves, bills folded between fingers of the other hand, the sweaty Marlboro matadors dirham-danced the slow single lane cars and rush hour pedestrians. A young wholesaler moved among them, replenishing supplies, dirham changing hands.

Marlboros, the universal currency. Someday, the UN will proclaim The International Marlboro Standard, with world currency and prices pegged to the Marlboro Market. Below, two go-go salesboys collided hurling themselves to a customer's car window. They laughed and patted each other as one made the sale.

Street vendor city here, a scrap of plastic on the sidewalk became a small shop selling jewelry and watches, leather things, shirts, jeans, snacks or plastic junk, even hand calculators and phones – PC's next?

A cardboard box on end, a Marlboro stand. Sans Moroccan tax stamps, $1.50+ a pack from down under the cardboard shop. Or 1 dirham for a single cigarette from the open display pack atop the box. So many young people doing this belied rich shiny mounds of fruit and veggies in the markets.

I laid this and other heavy raps, in what was fast mutating into Spanglish, on nodding, grunting Khalid heavy lidding the interminable long running event on the big screen below – with only two camera angles and no zooms or cut–ins to other events. Who were these fucking cheapskates ruining my life anyway?

Sucking sugary remains from the bottom of my cafe au lait glass, "Fuck it, I'm going."

Tangerino hand quicker than rising Americano head; sitting again, "No no, you must not leave your husband Khalid yet!" Twisting my watch arm, "Por Dios it's only 6 o'clock." Beguiling, low, "We will go to la coche again, my most adventuresome wife, and courageous Khalid will milk the giant red she-camel Por Dios! Have another cafe, wait until dark."

"Oh that scary Audrey Hepburn flick, no thank you very much, my Alan Arkin in black-leather jellaba. El honeymoon suite Renault is too hot and too fucking expensive for a knee-banger. I'm not a teenager anymore, at least my body. Plus I like real love, kiss and everything, not just more camelbullshit Tangerino!"

Both hands on, "I can do that! Last night en la coche, no TV, but tonight we have all this!" patting hard baby turd in pocket while squirming, sexually, I supposed. "I will do the Everything!" The Holiest of Holes?

Extinguishing the fire in both our eyes, "I've only got about 90 dirham in my pocket, putón (big male whore), and it's not to spend."

Tender earlips, "I know where we can go − the same abandoned house as last night, but not in the disgraceful coche, no no, but up on the second floor there are empty rooms where we can lie down, relax and do our everything Por Dios!"

Whispering tongue in my skeptical ear, "Tonight I surrender my Marhueco manhood to you, my first and only husband. Your only wife forever, brave Khalid, pleasure mount the giant red he-camel Californiano!"

His tongue fucking my ear and finger pressing between my cheeks on chair made me glance at the few other balcony TV watchers slumped around their tables. But they to a man were zapped to scantily-clad women in color interminably running on the other TV.

23

A shred of Saliva common sense pulled my wet ear away and removed his pumping hand from between the cheeks of my ass in the plate glass window; thank god people don't look up.

Frugal Kansaño farmer, "No deja vu's por favor, I can't afford them."

Hurt dark dagger stare as I coolly excused myself for the baño nearby, another advantage of the drowsy TV section. As usual, the Tangerino restroom was spanky and odorless, with those handy little concrete feet, direction depending on fuction, for males that is. I was still facing forward most of the time, gracias a dios. And a small plastic bucket under a faucet for flushing and general cleaning-up fun.

Back at our table, I picked up Boris and Gorby's George Washington beauty competition in my *International Herald Tribune* and white A's cap to shield poor pale (red actually) face from the hateful sun, go away.

"Yeah, I'm going home, etc. Tired and doan wanna spend any more dirham."

Khalid stood up, agitated, "But I have no plans tonight, reserve all my time for you. And I say you I promise to do the Everything Por Dios with you my only wife, for La Palabra Es La Palabra!"

Grunt, "I'm not Mrs. Khalid yet, ese."

Worried, "You want to buy some TV?" whipping out baby turd. I snort-declined, for I still had pages to go in my own TV Guide.

Standing close, suffering, "I don't have any dirham, you give me some for coffee tonight." I handed him a purple ten dirham bill with the King on it, worth more than a dollar.

Angrily waving it, "What the fuck can I do with 10 dirham?! Give me 20 more at least Por Dios!"

Biz smile, "I know it's not much for a whole hour of your valuable time, my busiest Khalid, but then you didn't have to do anything but run your mouth – or do you charge by the word, mi Señor Bueno Italiano?"

Pulling back, frightful black eyes, "Don't insult me my evilest wife, I Tangerino man! For the love and trust between husband and wife is the most precious gift – "

Gentle hand on face, "I'm sorry Khalid, but I can't. We spent too much last night so we don't have today," a fact that Khalid and governments around the world blithely disregard. My hand dropped, standing close, waiting.

Noble low voice and eyes, "I am most lamentedly sorry about the 200 dirham of last night. Honest Khalid never do that again to you Por Dios, my most rememberful wife."

Light laughter pulled off, gracias goddesses, "Que será pues – chiao cabrón (asshole)."

I patted startled Khalid goodbye on my way to the stairs down to pay the waiter 10 dirham for two cafe au lait plus tip, and leave disappointment behind – for he was a sincere funny guide but guiding too many of my dirham into his idleness habit – I wired eyes with a fellow balconian, toasted, hairy-chested, sprawling open-shirted on his small stool. But it would have been too tacky to do anything more with poor Khalid standing there staring at his 10 dirham bill.

When I was sure he wasn't following me on the slow sidewalk, I jumped over into the street – the fast lane for breathing and long free strides down to Tanger Bay for filling, perfect cous-cous poulet with a cerveza Speciale for 30 dirham plus tip. A change from the tinned anchovies and sweet natural yoghurt on French bread for lunch in my humble hotel TV room.

Más gusto than taste, quick divorce.

But of course it was not to be, for worm and screw must grind till same. At 5 p.m. the next day, our special time as designated by you-know-who, the hotel desk clerk called my room to announce the faithful arrival of same.

"¡Yo Bajaré En Un Ratito Muchas Gracias!" ("I'll be down who-the-fuck-knows-when thanks!"), I screamed into the phone, a heavy black wall job above my bed with weak reception from the ancient cord switchboard downstairs. Slow discouraged clothes jump and A's cap, cramming so much shit in blue Benetton's baggy pockets (I had two pairs, washed them on me in the shower). Down the old hall of lemon and lightest mint trimmed in black enamel. Down the corkscrew marble staircase foot-sculpted in the middle, flipflops clacking.

He was sitting in one of two comfy chairs by the reception desk no wider than the long entrance hall lined with small real plants; Tanger had smart taste, Moorish, French, Arab, what?

His tasteless bravado laughter in a cloud of Marlboro smoke, bragging in Arabic with two desk clerks; what was he telling them about me anyway? Clean, neat Khalid slowly rose, greeting me with a rusty it's-a-new-day smile; he did look nice today.

I the required grinny polite to clerks, "Muy buenas tardes eses, qué onda pues amigazos locochones," handing the sexier one my room key and 3-D eyes on a platter. Flowery farewells, Khalid calling them by name — they must know everything, even la coche?

Oh well, they probably suspected even worse, so being a normal faggot TV fan made me an honorable man here? Anywhere?

Stopping Khalid halfway down the hall, I gestured to the idle clerks, and in Saliva H.S. cheerleader captain's voice, en español, "Khalid, my highest friend, did you tell your buddies over there that you're taking me home tonight to meet my nueva familia Tangerina?" (Discreetly omitting belt dowry and din.)

All laughed, Khalid embarrassed(?) but he boasted to the clerks in Spanish, for my benefit, that he was conveying onto me this rarest opportunity to experience the beauty

26

in my own eye of the real home of a real Marhueco family, for I was no ordinary tourist Por Dios.

Appreciative nods and murmurs from the desk clerks as we walked alone together out onto Boulevard Pasteur, elegant crowded tourist trap, up a shady side street for private negotiation. As usual, black birds at dusk were screaming in the trees; what were they, anyway?

Sweating, purple bandana working, "Why you say them that my lyingest wife?! I tell you too much relative in my house, you understand Spanish Por Dios!"

Softest, sincerest blues lapping angry blacks, "Because I don't believe you, Khalid."

Whirling away in disgust, "Fucker motherfucker! Not believe your fucking husband fucking Khalid's anything!" Wheeling in challenge, "All right fucky know-everything man, I take you to my fucking house, see whole fucking family fucker!"

Soft hug, "Oh gracias, sweet Khalid — and your Spanish is getting more Mexicano everyday!"

Grunting, he led me up the shaded sides of treed bird screaming streets I soon recognized from la coche night. Yes, Khalid bad rich kid. But not hiding his face today for we were spaced single-file in our spy routine, looking for enemy agent faces under lovely jellabas. Fast down a small walled cul-du-sac, together through the rusty squeaking gate, the dead house gaping windows.

I stopped, "Uh, Khalid, does your family live in l'thicket Renault?"

Pulling me in, "Hurry so no one will see us. Here first our Everything, then I take you to my home Por Dios!"

In hot house with walls on floor, dogshit smell missing, as were the stairs to the second floor. "Follow me!" he hissed, outside through a small courtyard, over heaps of plaster and sticks.

Khalid scrambled atop a seven foot white wall, then helped me scrape bare-legged up it, rubber-soled flipflops gripping heroically. Whoops, a couple of feet farther down on the other side.

Hushed, "Quick!" He dropped down into a pile of sticks crashing (must be a fuel storage place). I let myself down, scraping the wall, into his strong sweat-slippery arms, with most of the wall's whitewash on my shirt, shorts and legs. Khalid had not a whit on him – well, he'd lived here longer and had probably been chased by the cops a lot more, plus we had cars back in Saliva.

"In here!" Into a doorless room with blissful marble steps we slipped up. Plaster off the upstairs wall, bare studs, slight musty smell, no glass in windows but no breeze, damned August heat bouncing off the flat roof above our heads.

I stood gasping, mopping sweat rolling face and neck, futilely slapping whitewashed clothes and legs. Khalid found a mini straw broom in a small tiled room off the plundered bath. He swept the long closet(?) room and shook out three long strips of heavy brown paper. Such a clean trick, but Arabs are, they say.

Motioning me to sit and share a Marlboro on our rude paper bed, backs against the wall. Khalid smiling satisfied, black eyes alive, "Much more beautiful here than la coche, no, my most athletic wife?" taking my non-handkerchiefing hand.

"Yeah, it's the fucking penthouse! I don't know, Khalid, it's so hot up here, I feel a little funny – "

Khalid's kiss surprised me, soft at first, then in for the kill as new lovers felt and pushed in natural sweat lubricant amazement. And the tooth gaps were delicious!

Falling, twisting off clothes on brown paper, mouths eating, camels cock-fighting, KY fingers praying deeply in our holiest of holes, when Khalid slowed, then stopped. I felt his squat dark camel dying on my white Saliva belly.

Gently rolling out from under, our greased fingers retreating, at ease. Soft kisses and reassurances, "Oh who

28

cares, Khalid? Por Dios I can still fuck you. Ha, just a little joke. Seriously, it's happened to everyone, putón (can be a term of affection), to me, even to your ancient fathers, I bet. Your father! How can we go to his house with my clothes all fucky and whitewashy?!" desperately fumbling the sweaty KY mess beneath us on damp brown paper, and covertly checking my wallet and folded bills in twisted Benettons.

Khalid mourned my tender hugs, "Now you think your husband Khalid not real man because he afraid of angry red he-camel, my largest wife. Look at you," fondling my moaning camel twitching for a home. "Por Dios, Californiano pussy man more man than strong Marhueco youth!"

While I recited to easily-impressed Khalid the We're All People, We Don't Measure Love Tape, I ran a video of the real baños turqueños through my mind to keep my camel in business. Sticking its greased nose between Khalid's facing hairy thighs tightening muscularly helped too.

Of course, ask at the hotel desk. I requested a sauna and jacuzzi place, but they knew — for I hadn't asked where the local whorehouse was, and they'd probably seen too much of puto Khalid. A couple of blocks from my hotel was los baños turqueños turísticos. Modern wood and tile, hot blast showers, then a friendly man scrubbed me in a private washroom, and escorted me into a dizzying steamroom and draining wood sauna, more slow showers, no jacuzzi. (Be sure to get the massage special and tip generously.)

Before I knew it, I was gasp shouting, my angry camel thrill-spitting past Khalid's holiest of holes right onto my 49'ers Super Bowl XXIII t-shirt. Eat your heart out, Sam Wyche.

By now, passion pro Khalid was resurrected, his KY'ed camel sliding my hairy pussy belly. He skillfully fulfilled my almost everything with his small but long distance camel, snugly Trojanezed despite his groaning protests. But when the Trojanenz was on the other foot, so to speak, camel victim's terror abated only when he was allowed to timidly sit on it, after vigorous rimming and fingering, of course, and slide himself down at our mutual breath-sucking pleasure while I fondled the front of him sitting before me. My everything slipped up his tightness, stopping, thrill welded together at last.

"If you feel like the back of your head is flying off, you know it's a damn good fuck," Emily Dickinson was right! as he crashed hard fuzzy buns against my maniacal Salivan thighs. My greaseball hands fought his aroused hairy camel, until scream explosion in Trojanenz and dark camel's milk slapped my gasping, licking face.

There was the new fuckbuddy closeness in the sweat dripping cigarette after, sprawled together on destroyed clothes, sturdy brown paper smeared but intact, wallet and money still OK.

Languidly tonguing giggling tooth gaps again, "And now what, pues?"

"Ah my mightiest wife, we go to our favorite hamman to cleanse and purify ourselves after our desperate act of wedded love. You like how strong husband Khalid slay fierce red he-camel he still feel in him forever?" fondling my drowsy pink wrinkledness.

Reciprocating, rubbing dozing dark camelito (little camel), "Yes, mighty he-camel sleeping deliriously now, but how good the rest of me feels depends on your hole price."

Thick tan fingers choking sleeping camel, tenderly, "Ah my most suspicious wife, Por Dios you are still angry about the 200 dirham of so long ago. So I give to you for free Por Dios, this my very first surrender of manhood love to the most special man ever come into my poor lonesome life, only 150 dirham!"

Snoring camelito Tangerino rudely awakened by rearing

red camelón (giant camel), "How about 100 dirham, your fucking cabroness, and I pay for los banós y el jugo de naranja?"

Tongue fucking erotic tooth gaps preceded the next round of the camel fight on slippery brown paper – the little dark guy didn't stand a chance Por Dios!

You can actually do quite a lot at the hamman, in a dim tiled washing cubicle down at the end, around the corner – just like the gay action section at nude beaches back in La-La Landia. We soaped in new fuckbuddy intimacy under slick underwear in postcum admiration play, new lover doing exactly what he wanted, to the other's delight.

Then fresh squeezed OJ, lounging TV underweared on the old locker room bench, Tanger the center of the cosmos for a minute.

"And now, a tu casa pues?"

"Oh, what is the late hour already, my too tired wife?"

"I don't know, my watch is in the locker. You think it's too late to go to your house tonight?"

Actually, the fuck wall had been enough. I wanted to be fresh and perky for my Moroccan housewarming, not all fucked-out with TV antenna bent. And my clothes so white-stucco'ed they looked like I'd flunked the wall-climbing test for my Tangerino burglary license. What would his father say, his mother think?

Khalid never mentioned his home or family again. I said nothing – he never asked me how many $100 travelers checks I had – why push reliable fuckbuddy bicamel best friend?

ABDVLLAH

He was too beautiful to look at, so instead I plagued listless Khalid in our belabored español, becoming more intelligible now that we were best fuckbuddies.

"So Khalid, my most learned political prognosticator, what do you think Morocco's chances are of getting into the European Free Trade Zone in say the next 20 years of your puto life?"

Eager Khalid ready, "Hah! Por Dios, Marhuecos not even in Europe pues, my most geographically confused wife."

"Simón, I know that – "

"And why you say 'Simón,' man's name?"

"En Mexicano, Simón means 'fuck yes,' like nil means 'fuck no.' Don't you remember your new Mexicano vocabulary words in your burned-out TV circuitry?"

Heehaws as Khalid went over it all in Arabic with precious gem Abdullah, his friend we'd run into, although Precious Gem spoke nearly flawless though slow español and understood me perfectly.

But they enjoyed their stories redigested here, like good Midwesterners, and their animated Arabic conversation gave me reason to deep-breathe Abdullah's lean dark brownness, bold eyebrows touching Roman nose, ebony lashes butterflying his shocking green eyes, thanks to the cultural hodgepodge that is Tanger, and even musically-laughing clean intact teeth.

He was intelligent and had a great personality, too. I could tell by how he had yelled at and mocked Khalid in Arabic, something about dirham, hah! poor Khalid squirming soft piteous excuses. Funny but polite to me, his many faceted emerald eyes deep-set under dark jutting brow, withdrawing introspectively when Khalid's normal raucousness rocked the small cafe stool Abdullah clung to

— oh please goddesses, let me be his stool tonight!

"And, and listen, Khalid — Khalid! How about Turkey getting into the E.C. first, it's part in Europe and part in Asia — " but they were long gone into Arabic, my usual Tangerino experience in crowds larger than one. My question was really an attempt to impress haughty(?) Abdullah; he seemed to condescend to limited Khalid, what must he think of me?

Abdullah passed his fat TV snack — did they all carry those plastic-wrapped hard baby turds in their pockets? — around the dingy cafe's only outdoor table made of stacked concrete blocks. It was near the ancient Medina's Arab maze neighborhood where I prayed to live if I ever had my fucking job interview. Oh well, fun vacation, at least today.

Love's lucky magnet had drawn Khalid and me to magic Abdullah watching "a friend's" Marlboro store, a wooden vegetable crate on end with open Marlboro box on top, a few feet from our table on the edge of the street. But there was no sidewalk nor street for they were one without cars, a few dusty pedestrians trudging by.

Occasionally, a passer-by took a Marlboro from the pack and dropped a dirham coin, 11¢, on the box, relaxing Abdullah not bothering to retrieve them.

Shaking Khalid over our block table (lucky Abdullah was in the middle), "Khalid, Khalid! So how much can a Marlboro salesperson earn in a day? How much do they pay for each pack wholesale?" (Business fun like sports.)

Khalid laughing back to español, "Maybe he pay 100 – 120 dirham for a carton of ten packs. But they not make their money from cigarettes, no no, Marlboro pack on box means the everything for sale here Por Dios!"

Abdullah's young giggles shook his long shiny black kinky ringlets I wanted to sperm all over in; my sperm vessel's rising abetted by Abdullah's chummy leg rubbing bare mine, and his long, brown fingers gracefully weinering

33

his Coca Cola bottle and glass as he poured it over a lemon slice, foam perfectly reaching the top. I always ran mine over and who cared what boring Khalid did?

My companions had followed my lead when I'd ordered a Coke for a hot afternoon respite – plus possible rumbling stomach remedy – back in Saliva they say it kills everything. Everybody knows about that nail experiment in the science class, or was it nutrition class? Or perhaps an emergency douche experiment in Drivers Ed?

Restless Abdullah now indulging himself in a common male public practice here: scratching his tasty eggs and crunching his slim jim under his tight worn, flowered slacks. Oh goddesses, please make me concentrate on Khalid's dominating voice, his emotional lilting Arabic sounding so Italiano with constantly moving face and hands driving me crazy already!

Jolly Khalid probably wouldn't mind my escaping with willing(?) Abdullah; he was used to dealing with my type. Just today, Khalid had humorously guided me to two gay bars in the South of Pasteur (SOPA?) district in the blistering sun (it was cool in my hotel room, shaded by a tall building 15 feet from my window, so like a lucky fool I came out).

One bar wasn't open yet; the other had a large sign outside, RESTAURANT; inside, a spacious nondescript tabled room. Khalid promptly seated me in the corner at the end of the bar, he sitting on the outside "to protect delicate Americano wife," back to that shit.

Protect me from a few older Moroccan men with a handful of dudes interspersed, standing with their backs to us at the other side of the L-shaped bar, fully mirrored, ideal for cruising?

The bar's high old walls adorned with posters of poor Marilyn Monroe trying to keep her skirt down, and Judy Garland sucking mike. And several indistinct caricatures – Truman Capote? Somerset Maugham? Barbra Strei-

sand? Where were Oscar and Walt W.? Yep, the icono-
graphy was correct.

Even King Hassan II was there in photo, white military
uniform but with a rakish grin for the boys. Damp
bandanaing face and neck, I nudged Khalid, indicating the
few customers slow social intercoursing with their backs
to us but dark eyes interested in the long mirror. "Do you
think they're discussing how much they'll pay for my great
white Americano zep (cock in Arabic)?"

Khalid rocked his barstool laughing, slapping my
shoulder too hard, "Hah! Thieving putos there planning
to rape you, steal all your dollar – but don't say that word
in public, I shouldn't teach you Arabic, you disgrace your
protector Khalid!"

Pushing him back, his bar stool rocking more, "Bullshit
mierda. Everybody already knows the truth about you and
me, or me and any man younger than 100 I'm with here.
So might as well face reality, my blindest wife Khalid, and
enjoy it."

Khalid's nervous encounter with reality laugh, "Here
the bartender, we order now Por Dios."

Tall, Adams Family pasty bartender darkly chuckled
my español order of dos cervezas Speciales, the cheaper
local brand – beer's all the same shit, come on!

The slow motion 'tender humorously put on a reggae
cassette Khalid had taped at a friend's today – slow
dreamy, pattery drums. Khalid boasted he'd bartendered
at so many Tangerino joints that he knew all the bartenders
in town! I feigned being impressed, though 'tenders do
know all the underworld haps, they say.

We dumped Speciales in glasses, slugged, bliss. I was
using the glasses now in spite of water drops in them,
everyone else did and it seemed the least I could do. I
didn't wanna be a fussy one who acts extra nice just cuz
they're in another country. If I couldn't kinda be me, I'd
stay home en La Missión, ¡Donde Está La Acción! Plus holy

35

Imodium cheap here, $2.75 for 20 capsules.

"You come here 11 or midnight, many men." Expansive wave, "Place full the every friendly man."

"Oh you come cruising for dirham here a lot, my hottest little wife?"

Easy chuckle, "My friend all tell me."

Nodding at the skeleton in black and white a safe distance away, "Did you zep the bartender yet?"

Bending-over laughter, "Shhh Por Dios! His zep for you not me!"

"Well, necrophilia would be a new kick, but necrophilia's better with my shyest wife Khalid."

Shoving me nearly off high stool, "You better learn to fuck live ones right first Por Dios!"

Self-congratulatory laughter at our coarse wit, Khalid mixing baby turd crumbles with Marlboro for gay TV break with our Speciales.

"And the fucking is upstairs, I presume?"

Professional guide, "Oh but of course, do the Everything here," as he greedily sucked another dying baby turd.

A ver – . At last I paid for the beers plus a generous tip to the grinny corpse behind the bar. Khalid collected his reggae tape and we left, to strollburn towards the ancient Medina and his friend Abdullah sitting perfectly alone there.

And I now slipping in lust on my hard, small stool under a rickety beach umbrella stuck into the pile-of-blocks table. Too hot, too twitchy, trying to force myself to stop light scratching the sweat-irritated mosquito bites on my legs and feet. Khalid had felt them and laughed, right on Le Boulevard, comparing my bare Benettoned legs to a beautiful woman's, "Slim shape, blond hair, very white."

"White my ass, I'm red!" dragging Khalid through slow traffic to the shady side of Le Boulevard. "You don't know how we poor white people suffer, scalded by your satan sun! Next life, I'm gonna be lucky brown like you."

Slapping my arm, "Hah! You be black like Sudanese!"

Slapping back, "Fuck off I hope so, soul bro."

Maybe just a few quick handkerchief swipes to remove sweat tickling puto bites. Scientific fact that mosquitoes and other suckers prefer the virgin blood of Bay Areans, we don't have them there. Mosquitoes were rare here, the fucking, lying tour books said back in virgin Frisco, but of course the International Mosquito Conspiracy met rare me at the boat.

Kicking at flies tormenting my flipflopped toes, they weren't bothering Khalid or Abdullah — too much protein in my Saliva blood?

A cigarette customer plucked one from the open pack, picked up the few dirham coins from the trusty vegie crate, and walked over to our block table. Handing the coins to Abdullah, they spoke quick conspiratorial Arabic. Casual chest slap goodbye, the man was out of sight up the dusty street, probably another baby turd magnate.

Expressionless Abdullah tossed the few coins into a brass incense bowl at the base of the table. It contained small change, a pack of Zigzags, a safety pin and one large button.

Leaning down, tipping the bowl to rummage, my strong chest against Abdullah's stronger flower-powered leg pushing back. Forced calm, "My, you do sell everything here, how much for this handy dandy safety pin decoration for your ear or nose?" posing.

Khalid quick, "Precious gem only 1,000 dirham!"

"¡999 y ni un centavo más!"

Reaching down, sweet laughing Abdullah playfully weinered my face and head with his elegant long digits. I resisted plowing my nose into his spread flowered trow so close as I tumbled the shining precious artifacts in Abdullah's perfect brass bowl. Oh farewell perfect new cocklove, I must rise now, straightening up and falling off

37

my stool, blood and god-knows-what rushing from my head, until Abdullah's heroic many-weinered grab saved my life.

Then he tenderly stroked my heaving Rambo Reagan-Saddam Bush t-shirt, admiringly, "Too funny, locochón." ("extremely crazy one," a Mexicano term of affection I'd taught them) "Where did you get that?"

Light headed, hysterically nonchalant, "Oh, uh er, in Califas (California), but I'm gonna quit wearing it, people already look at me too much here. Oh! I didn't mean you of course, Abdullah!" their hand-slapping laughter reddening my face redder.

"I—I like yours too," tracing my shaking fingers on his hard medium-hunky chest unfortunately covered by a green t-shirt, oh it matched his eyes! with a leather patch between the tits, and around it colorfully sprinkled designer names(?) I'd never heard of.

Intimate low sexy, "Gracias, locochón. Es Italiano."

"Oh, it's, nice too! Abdullah," forcing my weiners back to the relative security of mashing down my real weiner fighting Benneton and Hanes.

Breaktime, my straining blood sausage tucked, gracias a dios for baggy shorts. I confidently smiled and excused myself for the baño. Actually, I wanted to clear my head in inglés for a minute, and peek inside the low cafe where everything that could be was cracked, chipped or broken.

Wasted men, one woman, slumped mismatched tables and chairs. The young woman, in an orange ruffled dress, black permfluffed hair, looked angry, her large lips pursed in hurt? I shy-smiled her, not too encouraging, for what if she were really a puta (female whore) scheming for my American Express zep?

Here King Hassan in a weathered, dated photo with sensitive young artist look, hot! A few of the perkier patients began playing, Parcheesi? Of course my puppy had to come tagging along sooner or later, probably to protect me from the nodding patrons.

Proud Khalid introduced me as his best Tangerino amigo, making me mumble "fuck yeah" when he bragged he had taught me everything since I stepped off the boat, to the cafe owner, Khalid's dearest friend, no, more like a brother to him Por Dios.

Television career cafe owner, emaciated by Saliva standards, wizened dark wrinkled – and extremely frustrated that slow Americano could not understand his slurred English(?) lisped through no teeth. Didn't the cafe have a dental plan? He probably couldn't make it to the dentist office.

In laughing Arabic, cafe owner told Khalid, who provided simultaneous transtorture in español for me, about how he got busted, had to pay cops but they let him keep his TV. Big deal. But they were back into intense Arabic, yes! Romantic Americano slipped away to get to know his perfect Abdullah, alone at last, please goddesses, keep Khalid, now shouting, shouting till dawn!

Glittering emeralds approved my walking out of the cafe, drawn to them forever. I casually sat down, scooting my little stool even closer, first real smiles breaking – we knew.

His hand taking mine under the block table, serious español, "I believed you didn't like me, you hardly talked to me, you only talked to that stupid thieving puto Khalid, my best camel friend."

My free hand rubbing his rubbing mine under the table, "Oh Abdullah, you're too perfectly beautiful, I was afraid I'd cream my jeans, my shorts I mean!"

Tickling weiners jerked away, ice green eyes ablaze, "What you mean, locochón? I'm not beautiful, only woman, like Madonna, is beautiful."

Determined weiners reconquering his, "Beautiful can be both, as handsome can, my Perfect Abdullah."

Eyes wide, voice bittersoft, "My life not beautiful or

handsome — and perfect, hah! Look – " pulling his left arm away and pointing to a series of pink chocolate slash scars on his slim, brown inner arm.

Bending, kiss killing them softly, "I'm sorry, Abdullah honey. Can be a dangerous biz sometimes, I guess. At least they didn't get you with a gun."

Withdrawing his arm, back to hands gripping under table, "Guns necessary sometimes if you get big." Tossing his long dark kinks, Abdullah chuckled and cleared, his right hand weiners tightly encasing my throbbing heartbone disfiguring counterfeit Benettons.

His easy low laugh thrilling, "Your John Wayne pistola cocked and ready to shoot, locochón."

Wiggling on my cushy stool only made it worse, "And, uh, what about Kh–Khalid?"

After a reassuring Benetton pump, Abdullah returned his weiners to home before a terrible accident happened. He stroked his lengthening, running narrowly down his thigh, tight flowered trow stretch-smiling; proud perfect teeth, "Oh no problem dumping Khalid, we'll wait and say goodbye to him."

"But, uh, where?" forcing my eyes on new loveface instead of weiners long weinering worn love trow, so Abdullah retook my hands under table. Easy smile, "Oh no problem, I know where we can go. I have my own room very near here."

Straightening up on my stool, threatening hand squeeze, en español muy claro, "Exactly how many minutes –minutes, of very slow walking by mosquito-crippled foreigner in flipflops, to our perfect alleged lovenest?" for sometimes "close" meant miles here.

Not Kosher! Weinering around my sweaty handkerchief conveniently tucked between thigh and shorts, sensitive Abdullah, "Don't make paranoia, locochón. You've been hanging around with idiot camel Khalid too long. Don't worry, handsome woman, beautiful man, it's only a ten

40

minute crawl from here to my place through the Grand Souk (market) to the lower Medina."

The Medina, perfect! His long arm around me tight – oh no, not here! "I mean you really are locochón if you let Khalid's stubby little camel in your honeyed buns." Low, fast, "Did you touch his asshole, it's disgusting so hairy, how could you?!"

Pushing perfect love away so our body only lightly touched. "It's a polite Americano custom not to dish our tricks with a stranger, not till we're at least in bed."

Clever Abdullah laughed right away, then serious, "Actually, I appreciate raggedy-ass Khalid for his natural surrealism, and his instinct to always lie first, worshipping his pretended suffering until it has become real – a typical pathetic victim of our real and now neocolonialism."

I agreed! What a cool guy, but then I always was a sucker for psuedo-intellectual cute types with wit. And scars on his arm? Oh well, probably just from a Coke bottle. Khalid had told me that if I really wanted to get someone, I should hurry and buy a large Coke, break the bottle over my enemy's head, and go for his face. Thus some Tangerinos sported face defense scars on their arms.

I informed Khalid that we Americanos didn't fuck with Coke bottles, we had real guns. Eager Khalid really wanted to move there then – I recommended Washington D.C. for the complete arsenal.

Chipper Khalid back at our table, refreshed from his shouting. One look at us sitting there one and he knew. But Khalid good naturedly accepted the trick switch (he owed Abdullah money).

"So how much do I owe you Khalid for our little afternoon bar and Abdullah cruise?" whose love weiners were poking me delightedly under the table.

Proud Khalid, "Some guides say tat-tat-tat, tat-tat-tat, a certain price, but not Honest Khalid, no no. I say let the person decide, for in this world there are good men and

41

Por Dios bad men – "

"What's your Por Dios very bad man price?"

Laughing handslaps, "No no, you good friend, more like favorite brother to me."

"This afternoon I was your most delicate Americano wife – does this mean we're drifting apart? And what was that shit about your wife two kids needed milk the first night at the hamman?"

Abdullah's thigh squeeze under the table, yes we'd do this forever, his guffaws shaming poor Khalid. Real or imagined past grievances are a fun bargaining tool, but I laid a 100 dirham bill on the table for Khalid. He was impressed cuz he knew I couldn't afford it with what was coming, but I'd be firm with my perfect love Abdullah.

Cocky, "Come on Khalid, my most impoverished husband, it's fight time. Tell me how you must have 200 dirham for your milk-sick children. Knowing you, you'd spend it to milk this – " tugging his drowsy zep through his dull 501's.

Khalid amusingly thrust his Levied zep about on his stool, and several weird looking stragglers – for what normal person is out in 90 degree heat – shuffled towards our little circle jest, laugh-remarking in Arabic, hands on zeps. Split time.

Abdullah grabbed Khalid's 100 dirham bill from the table and stuffed it into his pocket, pulling me away. Off to the screaming races in Arabic, old zep men retreating, Coke bottles gone, I noted with relief.

But it was just a typical mouth fight, Abdullah culminating in español for my benefit, "You lazy worthless piece of wet cameldung, this is fucking August, the high fucking tourist season so you get your disgusting hairy asshole down to the dock and get those tourists coming off the ferry hungry for a little reasonably priced domestic TV! And then you can pay me some more – I was an idiot to give you credit!"

Khalid bled broken black eyes at me. Airily, "Gee, Daddy Khalid, can I borrow the keys and condoms for tonight?"

Shattered Khalid stalked away, saving his face with rude Arabic gestures and curses. I knew I'd feel guilty later about my cruelty to him, but it felt so good at the time that I just fucked the guilt as I had learned in Califas.

I paid the young scuz waiter 12 dirham plus tip for Cokes, fished lemon slices out of our empty glasses and juiced puto bites, neat stinging sensation overwhelming itching for a minute.

I slapped on my damp salty A's cap for heroic trek from under the beach umbrella into the slanting sun to help Abdullah, satisfied and mumbling, close up his store. He pocketed the partial pack of Marlboros and carried the crate to beside the cafe, ignoring the incense bowl by our star-crossed block table; maybe we'd have it bronzed someday. I followed him, perfect peach gazing — not one of those tragic but all too common skinny Arab asses, but more a plum firm Asian one — Mister Jade Eyes Perfect Golden Mountains.

Abdullah and I strolled close without words, after I thanked generous Khalid in absentia for his 100 dirham lifetime subscription to laughing new love, who agreed to everything from kiss to holiest of holes, yes!

Across the busy Grand Souk market, its round grassy plaza filled with pedestrians, slow car traffic and shops circling it, a tall mosque tower, and high white keyhole arches into the Medina. Under an arch, this way and that through crowds on pedestrian-only streets, then up a street of steps I imagined Roman soldiers cruising Perfect Us on (we turned them down flat, crude beasts).

We attracted but a few languid looks from weary Mediterraneans, watching it all go round and round prairie farmers from Kansas again.

43

PERFECT ABDULLAH'S VACATION

Curving up ancient Medina stone footpaths past tiny shops selling everything for tourists and neighborhood residents, finally my new best friend Abdullah, spoke, "Aquí." (here)

Slim brown Abdullah handed me an old key and indicated one of a pair of battered wooden doors, his light español with an edge, "Mi casa es tu casa, you open it."

"Ha, I wish!" silently congratulating myself for smoothly inserting the old brass key into the worn door, turning it correctly the first time away from the other double door without betraying lust run amok in my baggy blue shorts, nervous flipflops twitching.

The open door threw a shaft of sunlight across the clean concrete floor up the peeling back wall two meters away. Abdullah led me into his simple cell and lit a white taper in a ceramic candleholder with Moorish designs I prayed to for the strength and easiness of another True Love Lust, but always The First Time for trembling Saliva Mind Virgin.

I closed the door, threw home the heavy bolt lock and pocketed the old brass key, mi casa pues. The bedside candle illuminated a large single platform bed which took up half the room with space barely to walk beside it, and small ornate wooden shelves above the bed with many impressive books and other fine junk.

The windowless cracked mint walls had slick posters of candle-shadowed blond surfers, motorcyclists in black leather, Playboy centerfolds, ahem, and Madonna playing mean; no mirrors. The candlelight couldn't reach the high ceiling lost in the dark to a spider world probably. The high ceiling and thick mud walls kept Abdullah's perfect room cool in the late afternoon fucker sun. I was barely handkerchiefing after the short walk from the slow friendly cafe pick-up with my ex-best fuckbuddy Khalid, who was probably hustling TV tourists now for dirham, or a bottle of Johnny Walker con pussy.

Abdullah motioned for me to sit on the bed, firm but soft, like me pues. His long slimness sat beside me on the sturdy bedspread, a fine, red-striped killum (Berber weaving).

With ass bouncing abandon, "Por Dios a real bed! Didn't know you used them here."

Cruel Abdullah's jest in español, "I thought you enjoyed la coche pues – chingón locochón (fucking nut)," mocking my Mexicano; I could use a little more pseudo and a little less intellectual quickness right now.

My sorrowful arm around him, twitching on the edge of the bed, "Oh that chingonazo blabby Khalid told you everything, even about the wall too, I suppose!"

Nodding his black kinky ringlets I played in by shiny candlelight; serious, "Be careful locochón, la policia look at men with whitewash and stucco dust on their clothes. You must learn to scale walls, mi amigo, without disgracing yourself."

Formerly worshipful hands dragged yelping thick ringlets down on the killum, "Fuck you very much my smartest-ass spiritual master Abdullah, but frankly I don't see much future in wall climbing for a Kansaño boy. There, we climb civilized barbed wire fences."

Wiry Abdullah squirmed away, standing, mashing shadowed kinks back to disorder, "You are a funny and half-wise man. That's why I chose you for tonight."

"Gee thanks – which half?" Abdullah's low laugh was home. "Well, I guess that's not too bad for a barefoot boy from Castro Street."

Lust shoved poor Love under as candle-shadowed stripteaser Abdullah kicked off his sandals and pulled his t-shirt over jiggling ringlets. Slow candle strobing lightly muscled flexed chest with tight black curls on nips and pecs, my eyes flying down fine hairs to manly belly button to wiry black massing flowered trow unzipping, underwearless.

Oh it was so soft thin long, Muslim-cut of course, with doorknob head, crowded outwards by dos huevones putones del gran ranchero hanging low, dark springy jungle bush to lose my face, my life, in.

Abdullah light, "You want to see the back now?"

"Ow!" He hung his clothes with many others on hooks on the double doors, his poor flowered trow finally freed from too taut seam-threatening weinerhood, relaxing on their hook till noon mañana, I prayed, while dying of plump peaches poisoned delight by shadowed candlelight.

Love bouncing back in español, "Hey come on, Perfect Abdullah, you sure ain't no fuckin' wham bam thank you man one night stand, I think I really love you, really really really, you know?"

Casual "Simón" as he sat down against me, then lying back, yes! Thick black underarm pussies, muscular legs parted, displaying on his curly dark thigh an already alarmingly long but slim, gracias goddesses, dagger, almost black, darker than the rest of him, graceful curved hardening, my first real Tangerino shafra (fierce Berber knife)!

Did he get bent like that as a moody adolescent bookworm whacking off 15 times a day in his locked bedroom, or behind the anatomy section of the Saliva Public Library? – oh no, that was me. The kid should be hot!

My clothes fell off, and kindly tofu brained, I took the cynical young puto into my understanding arms, pledging allegiance to Love again, "We need to talk, Abdullah."

Our desperate love cling fit perfectly, surely from another life. Together again, dark lite nihilist versus the only peace love pot hippie on my parents' Saliva farm in the 70's.

Abdullah moaned genuine(?) moans as he tongued my face, rolling on top, soft pushing his hardness already. But Love mightier than Lust rolled him off to side by side, soft faces, but we continued humping, his greased electric eel burning blond hair off my deathgrip thighs.

Barely gasping, "Let's be real, Abdullah my greatest love." Sorrowfully, "Hey man, I know this is all imperialist – you Arabs are nice but prickly people who have been run over by Europeans too much, who even drew the maps of your fucking countries. But outside of that, in the cosmos, where only the spirits live, I love you there as we love each other in Tanger, our center of the Universe."

Snorting, hard curved leg-jabbing, "Oh, so our prominent civic booster Khalid has shown you his pornographic satellite photos."

He stopped, his thin strong arms around, squeezing my ass too hard, "Real is, you've got the dollars locochón, and I'm the Third World puto, your 'perfect love' for one many–dirhamed night, hah!"

Choking inside at his vicious half-truths – for I had indeed been in perfect mutual love, even with Third World putos for – months at a time. And consecutively pues!

I executed a smooth pull-away to turn on the bedside battery boom box to Radio Madrid playing American, British and Spanish rockers. But I always switched the station whenever they played rap music in whatever language; finally, I could empathize with my parents' agitation at Alice Cooper and Deep Purple stirring up the termites in our white frame Saliva farmhouse during my teenage years.

Radio Madrid's deejays and news were good Spanish listening practice, but I wasn't listening today, I didn't care what they were saying about us as we lay there in imperalist impasse, hardongs twitching, beyond any helpful words I could conjure up in my love hollowed-out brain.

But our solemn minds were betrayed by our hearts of

47

the matter, greased and pushing against each other again, to a soft disco beat; I guess they call it dance music now.

Sliding against him, gesturing to the shadowed-moving walls, "I bet all the tourists you bring here must really dig your cool posters; they're 'a trip' as we say in inglés."

Weary only in voice, "I know trips — ácidos, cocaina, heroina, ópio," as he rose to his knees and gracefully pulled the heavy but not butt-scratchy red killum from under me. Then on black cotton sheets embroidered with red and yellow peacocks, he lay on top of me, playing grunting macho pig.

Into his delicious kinks, "So you bring many dirham lovers here, my pet Abdullah?" Quick laugh, "I mean it's all right and everything, for I'm a fervent worshipper of open relationships, as long as you don't let your loud obnoxious best friend Khalid and his dumb types in here."

Beautiful devil smile lying on mine, "No, only you come in my love-tent, my beautiful handsome wifehusband."

Fuck Love, I'd tried. So Lust in the saddle for the Kiss and Everything. Galloping to our Holiest of Holes, we dream slid into a religious procession, complete with Trojanenz and cream, Emily Dickinson's screaming heads flying off repeatedly.

After all probed and reprobed, we did eyes, wet soft snuggle kittens lapping Sidi Ali bottled water, pulsing candle kaleidoscoping gold brown gray flecks sparkling in Abdullah's green recessed eyes on my widely dilated blues, he told me.

Bright appreciative new fuckbuddy tone, "Smoke some kif, locochón?"

"Simón pues." Propped on elbow, stroking him, mine, all mine! "How long do you think our perfect love will last this brief lifetime together, my reunited Abdullah?"

Giggle stretching, lightly roughing me, "Hah, for you perfect love is all on the outside, like this!" wrapping his fuzzy legs around one of mine and humping it vigorously.

Firm nose slap, "Down naughty dog, down!" Abdullah became very excited and we began to tumble again. "Oh my incredible Abdullah, that was definitive proof that we've loved in other lives!"

Panting Abdullah giggled, "Dee-dee-dee-dee, Dee-dee dee," from El Twilight Zone. Proudly, "Yeah, I know all that Americano shit, I'm Culturally Conflicted, you know. Tanger gets six TV channels from Southern Spain, that's how most us Tangerinos learn español, aha!" pushing harder.

Groaning, "Oh thank you very much, Khalid, my lyingest tourist guide, plug your mouth now," lust tongues fitting perfectly.

When soreness of important parts poked irritated through our love(?)lust bliss, we were old enough to know it was time to stop for a minute. Merrily we washed each other by candlelight for Romantic Abdullah didn't use the kerosene lantern on the wall above his bed except for reading; amazing what you can accomplish in a small corner sink.

Clean procelain chamberpot with a snug lid for jagged postcum pissing, then warm intense naked close dancing, relaxing in Abdullah's timeless cell to mournful Moroccan music on, Radio Naccional? Surfers, motorcyclists, and playgirls of months smiled down on us; no wonder really sweet Madonna looked so pissed, watching bright young Abdullah throw away true love for cynical dirham lust.

Finally cross-legged Cub Scouts back on the bed, observing high merit badger Abdullah's little science experiment. A two foot long hardwood stick, the bark still on, with a sucking hole in one end and a tiny metal pipe on the other, which he dipped into green grainy kif from a round, pocket sized trimetal box of brass, copper and silver — los colores de los Tangerinos bonitos now all míos!

Abdullah reached to light his long mini-pipe, using the round box lid to dampen the glowing ember, he bogarting,

I with love's sincere arm around him, in español muy romántico, "My noble Abdullah, your deep green eyes of many colors delight my soul – wherever did you get them?"

Laugh-coughing sweet smoke, "Hah, mister romantic man," handing me the bark pipe. "My family fishermen for many centuries," chuckling, "and many ports, they say."

Back home I don't even smoke dope, except at parties, but in Marhuecos do as stolid Roman soldiers did, so I took a deep hit which threw me into coughing convulsions, my constricting throat trying to claw out of itself.

"¡Cuidado hombre!" helpful Abdullah warned, slapping my bent-over back, hurting it more. Breathe breathe, Sidi Ali gargle, then I took two tiny hits; who needed it here in the holy matrimony of love and lust?

"Your TV certainly gets bright reception," explaining to bemused Abdullah the TV-dope code from my ancient Saliva hippie days.

Serious, "Don't make paranoia, locochón. This is semi-civilized Morocco, not your Ronnie Ramboland. By the way, I'd like to borrow your t-shirt," leaning over to retrieve, wadded from the floor, my Rambo Reagan-Saddam Bush t-shirt with Scud missles bursting in air.

Friendly taking it from him, rewadding and throwing it back on the floor, "I love you, my precious life mate Abdullah, but we must have limits, so please fuck off – it's the only one I've got and everyone here wants it; I'm gonna quit wearing the fucker."

"Umm, 'fuck off' – nice talk for mister perfect love man," drawing deeply on his pipe again.

Dizzy, floating in each other on the narrow bed, so warm, my first Moroccan love home at last! "So your fisherfolk ancestors probably raped homeless Ulysses, and poor blind Homer – "

Mocking golden eyes, "And maybe even Cleopatra, and

Helen of Troy," glowing the ember in his bark stick.

Gentle back slap, "And the good Queen Isabella – "

Ember glow flying to eyes, "Hah! I leave that putaza católica for you, Mister First World white boy!"

Saliva H.S. drama class, 1974, original work, first performance in español: "I always assumed you were a racist, sexist, patriotic pig, but now a religious and class chauvanist too, my dear Mr. Nixon?!"

We laughed through the centuries forever in our soft candled cell, air perfumy kif, golden-haloed Madonna beatifically smiling her blessings down on us now.

"We Americanos are into mixed races you know, except for a few Klan cretins – we're a nation of fairly recent immigrants, so we haven't had time to learn to really hate each other yet."

Gold flecks glittering hard, "Except for your poor black people there."

"Simón, and the Indians too, not to mention Hispanics and everyone else. But it's happening for minorities, and for women too, too slow, motherfuckin' Republicans! Just like it's happening for us middle-of-the-road anarchists right here," climbing on his comfort chest, chewing tight curls, plead-mumbling, "Please please please love love love me me me!"

Play-laughing Abdullah kneeled over me and began slapping my face with his long, limber schlong. "You're too bossy, locochón. Khalid said you were mister know-everything man. I already quit school, daddy, why get degree then sit in cafes, why bother?" with an emphatic schlong slap to my mouth trying to bite his swinging, swelling tool of punishment.

"So what was, was your ma–major, Abdullah?"

Rotely slapping, "Arabic and French literature, hah. But now I've joined the real world of petty criminals and pretty putos all in a row."

He laughed louder, over Radio Madrid (Joe Walsh?)

51

as I writhed, hardened schlong slaps stinging my face redder. But our college days reminiscences were interrupted by yet another commercial message from The Perfect Lovelust Crusade for a Quasi-Sane Cosmos.

I don't know why my pesky sperm, with minds of their own, chose to jump on the six dark, even scars on Abdullah's inner forearm, but I politely began licking up my spilled leche promptly.

Dark laughter pushed my head away, "I charge extra for El Kink, mister Califas man."

So sincere I sounded hopelessly false, "I wanted to heal your gross outside scars to reach your sensitive inner ones, my sweetest long-suffering Abdullah."

Snarling, thrusting his scars in my face by harsh candle light, "How you think I got these fuckers?"

Nervous swallowing back to reality, "Uh, Coke fight, I suppose?"

"Hah!" Yellow hate eyes, "I had a messy war with myself and I almost won. Then they took me to the fucking hospital."

Oh no, oh goddesses, I didn't want to save him, I wanted him to save me. I didn't know what love was.

Calm breathing, "Oh my sweet confused Abdullah, you said you're only 22, god, a baby! Believe me, it's all so much easier and calmer when you get older and a little beaten down."

Flat eyes, voice, "I look too old to me already."

"Yeah, I noticed, no mirrors."

Proud, thrusting his scarred arm upwards, "These are my mirrors!" indicating Marlon Brando from "The Wild Ones" astride his hog on the peeling green wall in Tanger. "And that and that and that!" all of Abdullah's pretty First World dolls, posters in a row.

"Ha," my comforting arms around him, lying on soft black sheet with embroidered peacocks drowning in KY cum. "You remember in 'The Wild Ones,' Marlon goes in a restaurant in the little town his bike gang is terrorizing, and the waitress asks him what they're rebelling against. And Marlon answers, 'Whatcha got?' In a restaurant pues!"

Relaxed laughter, rubbing, green glitter eyes alive, gracias goddesses, I must be doing love again. "I mean, that's the heavy burden that youth must shoulder – to rebel and be crazy, and if you survive, then you can enjoy the comfortable status quo of the revolution you made in your minds."

Abdullah admiring something besides my tongue, cock, and ass at last! "You're an exceptionally blond, beautiful, funny Frisco bullshit man. What was it you do back in Califas pues, locochón putón?" (He was picking up Mexicano quick!)

"I'm Tangerino pues!" laughing our perfect fit of same size bodies in lovely different shades and proportions. "I mean I've been here for – several whole days! God, seems like several lifetimes already at least! Hey! Don't go Rod Serling on me again, puto cabrón!" sharp elbow in ribs preventing Dee-dee-dee-dee, Dee-dee-dee repetition.

Quiet candlelight story wrapped in each other, "My major was drama and fine arts and some other stuff back in Kansas, a farm state north of Texas where I'm from. But I was only half serious about too many things and never really learned anything, so now I'm a businessman."

Shaking ringlets howling against my chest, appreciative belly kisses, "Oh yeah Abdullah, a little lower please? Ah yes! Uh, yes, businessman – after I hitched through Latin America and collected weavings for myself and for gifts, and worked in some shops – Oh, Ah, Stop!" grabbing his black kinks.

"I don't wanna cum again so soon, I'm too old for this shit!" pulling his mouth up to safe blond belly button, while I continued reciting my resume into his cum-pungent pubes.

"So I'm trying to get a job here with an exporter

53

recommended to me back in San Pancho (SF) – if the fucker ever gets back from chingón Nueva York to hire me. So here I am, with the lucky love of my life; we've known each other long enough, Perfect Abdullah, marry me marry me marry me!" desperately chewing spongy pubes.

Yelping Abdullah jerked away, my head spitting black pubes, and wrestled me into quick submission. But he remained spread-eagle on top of me, just in case.

My mouth burrowed through his tangled sweat-scented ringlets, blowing his ear, "So tell me, sweet Abdullah, what is it you really want?"

Ditto in my ear, "Hah, mister stupid questions man."

Earlobe nipping, "Just getting down to basics. I mean if you really insist on marrying me and everything, I must know how to please my most imperfect Abdullah."

Resigned in my ear, "A beautiful, intelligent woman from good family wants to marry me. We studied in the university together, now she's a French and Arabic teacher."

"Ha, at least she's not sitting in cafes smoking her diploma."

"Too much work to be teacher, puto Marlboro man easier," fierce earlobe bite.

Jerking away, "Ouch, you fucker! Marry her, I don't care! Where's my mom Khalid to beat you up?!"

Asserting himself on me, mocking, "Our honeymoon very brief, mister bossy wife." Wearily, "But I can't marry, children, work work to get leche for children, lose my life, no I can't."

Sympathetic nose ear-burrowing again, "Oh, foolish child Abdullah, you never know what's going to happen until it happens and then sometimes you still don't know. As wise prophet Khalid says, 'Que Pasa, Pasa Putón. La Vida Es La Vida Pues.'"

Sharp on me, "Hah, more of Khalid's freeze-dried cameldung!"

54

"He's your best friend, he's just my fuckbuddy," test-biting his lobe.

"A clown, against the law for him to think. His hairy camel asshole will be deadmeat one of these days. And so will yours if you bite my putón ear any harder, my naughtiest child."

Pout, "But you bit me, real hard!" sticking my stinging tooth-printed earlobe in his stupid cat eyes.

Sucking my lobe, making it better, "That's different, you deserved it. I decide this lifetime, you get the next two. Fair, no?"

Earlobe snatched back, "Oh fuck you, you dominant faggot macho brute!" Bored yawn, "Have you got anything to eat, Abdullah? And don't forget, my bitingest wife, you've got quite the fuzzy welcome mat on your back porch yourself, so you shouldn't be throwing your camel turds at poor Khalid. How do you know about his extremely sexy hairy asshole anyway?"

Gripping me, "Oh, you did fuck him! But you didn't rim him – that's too disgusting! I mean you're so beautiful pink and blond back there and your mouth too, like Madonna – that's my positive Cultural Conflict."

"Oh, but of course!" More First and Third World sarcasm, cheer returned cross-legged on the bed with small moist cakes and agua Sidi Ali, embers glowing bark stick, new love's jagged edges smoothing into relaxed respect and easy impossible challenge. Candle out, we moved in sleep, moving us to sleep again, our perfect surreal lovelust too rich for real dreams.

Abdullah's sweating body lashing mine made me break through heavy kif-sex slumber to hear dull thumps. Abdullah muttered irritated French(?) stumbling to the door; I realized where I was, lovelust heaven my new address.

Abdullah mumbled, sliding back the heavy bolt lock

in the dark, and opened the door. Exclaiming an astonished "Ay!," stumbling backwards into the room, grunting, gulping, choking — I thought he was throwing up.

Then silence except for fast footsteps retreating down the night street. No, he wasn't throwing up, curled in a ball on the floor against the back wall, the still-open door throwing dim light askew on him. Oh god goddesses no!

Deep breathe, take over take over my inner voice, speak to me slowy clearly reasonably, in inglés. OK now, you must close and lock the door, now, get up now, off the bed, now! That's right, good, feets don't fail me now to door, fumble it shut and locked, good boy. Bad boy now it's pitch black in here and scared shitless! Breathe breathe on the door, he's lying dead there, no! Breathing, unbolt and open door a crack, they're not coming back, really. Oh dim light from the street, fast quiet feets to candleholder by bed, gliding now, automatic taking over. Oh traitor shaking hands drop lighter clanging rattling on floor, breathe breathe breathe — got it lit Simón cabrón, close and lock door. And approach it, Him, holding his candle before me. Candleholder set on floor his memorial, touching his curled brown warmth the easiest part, mouthing him soft cheerful sweet nothings, good good.

Breathe gently turn him over, no sound, black belly hair greased running candlelight scarlet, breathe breathe breathe breathe four this time, four means death in Japanese, glide breathing to shelves, if it's red lower the head if it's pale raise the tail, no that isn't it, red sails in mourning yes heavy books texts(?) heavy clothes from hooks trembling hands fold, press onto belly moving only rivers of scarlet books on top of folded clothes, pressure honey.

Don't go away, inner voice, outer taking over, kissing shadowed face, last tongue lust moving his like a ventriloquist's dummy, no breath. Finally I could ululate like good Arab wife over him, but softly, no they really won't come back really.

Small animal pain moan? In his face, "Abdullah!
Abdullah!" careful not to shake him and disturb clothes
and books compress, my hand on still chest.

Slow clear español in his face, "Abdullah, it's me, you're
OK! What should I do? Go to neighbors and call ambu-
lance, 911?"

Eyes still closed, agonizing moan, "Nooo!"

"Uh, uh, call a doctor? Uh — take you to hospital in
taxi!"

Painful low "No!", then he was still, my gentle shakings
to revive him fruitless. What-the-fuck-to-do panic time!
Khalid? Who knew where the fuck he was; where what
why the fuck am I? OK, I'll breathe — five this time, but
I could not feel my breath — should we die together? But
how? No, I was too Kansaño sensible, plus I'm afraid of
my parents.

Checked the books and clothes on him, already seeping
scarlet, stumbled into clothes from floor, door key
appropriately in new widder's pocket, no! Shake watch
on, Por Dios past midnight, watch wet. Get pillow and
killum from bed so he'd be comfortable, his head sticking
out of his red Berber tent.

Kiss kiss goodbye, no sign of breath. "I'll leave the
candle on next to your head, honey."

It didn't seem fair for me to selfishly deep breathe, but
maybe that was what he was doing now, watching his
candlelight funeral service as he floated to the top of his
former dark cell, up there playing with his spider friends
smiling down. So then why was Madonna screaming all
scarlet lips and Marlon crashing his hog through the wall?
I fled.

Casually looking wildly around, empty narrow night
street, shutters all closed, pale distant street light. Go
down, down, I remembered!

Soft, "Bye, Abdullah honey, I'll be right back." Fumble

57

locking the door, kissing rough wood numb to my lips, but I felt the hairy thrust against my bare leg. Gasping flipflops clambered up door nearly over roof!

A black and white cat out hunting; my soft trilled cat calls got it into my arms, a perfect centering device. Purring face to face, its green eyes glittering Abdullah-gold; I knew it understood why I kissed it and carefully positioned it to guard Abdullah's perfect crypt, no no, perfect lovenest, sobs choking from far away.

Clacking down deserted stone step street, Roman soldiers slaying crimson tides. My short scream startled me, as well as a jellaba'ed, veiled pedestrian popping up. Careful please, appropriate reality responses only on opposition turf thank you.

Yes yes, I was an eager tourist out for a brisk midnight military stroll, no silly cruising the merchandise, down bottom steps as fast as flips could flop, save him save me, maybe that's what love was, yes!

I fast slid crowds through a high keyhole arch to the Grand Souk market still going strong, full of midnight slow cars circling the pedestrian plaza.

But car lights, people, food stands all whirling too fast – Hitchcock merry-go-round, or poor Actors Studio Shelly Winters upside-down in the Poseidon again. No no, the reality was Abdullah running scarlet – breathe eyes closed, standing on the edge of Grand Souk street.

Now open, focus on the people, their features still blurred, squint breathe – yes! There he was!

The little Marlboro boy I bought packs from was darting around the outside of the Grand Souk plaza, where he had to run farther and expend more sweat chasing customers but escaped his larger competition. I always bought from him, of course, with my Americano penchant for the underdog, as long as he ran his ass off.

The gruff voice from the little boy's body was haranguing a customer to buy more; he was tough and street smart, plus the only one I knew here.

Dirty hands on, he persuaded his client to buy a carton which he miraculously whipped out of his skinny t-shirt under a voluminous shabby jacket. He quickly stuffed the 150 dirham from the sale into the side of his dirty sock, bulging with bills ("All tens!" he'd barked at my joking inquiry once).

His customer dismissed, he turned into me, instant smile, shake steadily his tiny blur hand, slap chests, "L'bas," (hello in Arabic), for I was a valued client, I prayed, "Hámdullah!" (Thank Allah)

In his raggedy street español, "Hi mister new Englishman, so happy see you again!" reaching up to pat my frozen shoulder.

New, yeah, didn't feel a day over 90. But it was calming to have friendly human contact with the other world, breathe cool – "Come with me!" in distinct decisive español, my hand gripping his non-existent shoulder under his baggy jacket. Back across Grand Souk street, dodging slow one-lane cars, under the large arch towards stone steps.

Jaunty, pulling me through the crowds, "Where to, Mister English? You want to buy carton tonight, maybe three or four – have for future!"

Future, shit. Goddesses forced concentrating in simple Spanish as we reached stone steps. I stopped him, bending down into his sweaty angel-devil face that was barely wavering now, "Listen my child, you're my most valued, trusted amigazo in the Grand Souk, and you must help your generous Mister English friend, no?"

For my tough slit-eyed Tangerino street boy, eagerly nodding in my power, would surely know a doctor who would come to treat an anonymous knife wound; oh!, for a few $100 American Express travelers checks, if –

Ragboy's grinning shrug, "Sure, my best friend Mister Englishman, what you need?"

My arm down on his padded shoulder as I started him up the deserted steps, "I know I'm taking you away from your business for a little while, so here's something for your time."

"Cool man!" his dirty little hand snatched the 100 dirham bill that should have been Abdullah's, oh. Carelessly wadding Abdullah's 100, he jump stepped it into his other, empty sock; no fool he, for I was a lot bigger than he was, and a lot younger too.

Confident shoulder squeeze, "And there will be more for you later if you do exactly what I tell you to," dragging him fast up the steps, no time for stupid Roman soldiers.

I leaned down towards his ear bobbing under stinky sweat-tangled dark hair, "Listen, my child. Mi amigo Tangerino is very sick and needs a doctor. I take you there now, then you go get doctor and bring him there – a doctor who asks no questions for dólares americanos."

He stopped at the top of the steps, under a street light attached to a house. Hard brown eyes slitting up at me, child's quavering español, "What happened to your friend, mister? Where the fuck you taking me, Englishman?!"

"Stomach problems, hurry!" I swept him around dim corner, double doors on the left. Street empty, damned cat had split, probably bored, you can never trust them.

Key yes, door open, boy hanging back – but Abdullah's candle was gone. Cigarette lighter lit – but nothing, no, nada, whadafuck?!

No Abdullah no scarlet no killum no compress books or clothes no scarlet floor. But I knew it really happened, the kif-sex delirium hadn't been that good, sorry Abdullah, yes it was, oh! "Abdullah?" I called softly.

I lit the cold candle back on the bedside stand to make sure – killum not on bed, only cum-stained sheet, everything clean and clear – reality check A-OK all wrong!

Gasping disbelief, I slumped on the bed. Madonna and Marlon said, did nothing but silently mocked me from their dirty, flickering wall, Madonna looking mean again. I'm sorry, Madonna, it's not my fault, I have no scarlet on my hands, I didn't even touch him there.

I couldn't feel white candle wax, so fascinating, splish splashing my ma-moving hands, Abdullah would be so proud of me − no, I wanna go home!

Boy in, door closed, bolt banged; confidently, "Your sick friend got better quick."

Numb on dead love bed, crazy feeling sorry for poor kid, he must think I'm nuts sitting here trembling, candle in front of my face. I must look like Dracula strobing on Quaaludes. That's not even funny, locochón, oh.

Think thank thunk: he couldn't have left here under his own power, someone came and got him and cleaned up the scarlet. Were they watching me leave, or us come back? The cat split to warn us − I know nothing, nada.

Husky voice out of darkness, "That's not why you brought me here, Mister English."

Taking the candle from my dead hands and setting it on the bedside table, the Marlboro boy flopped flat nude on the bed beside me. His baby fingers beat an amazingly long hairy cock for such a little guy!

Whirling candle–shadowed seductive español, "I like make much milk in foreigner's mouth. Only 100 dirham more for strong young Marhueco hot boy, mucha leche fill Mister English mouth. Only 200 more I fuck your white ass, then you have me for future. Every night I be your fuck son, mi nueva papá inglés!"

Gleefully humping against me sitting there, "Big hot brown banana, much hair on young boy, you Englishes like, no? Boy's banana all yours now," expertly jacking my hand up and down his jumping dirham bone.

I came alive. As the hardong is yanked, the man or boy follows; I jerked him startled off the bed into his protesting filthy clothes. "My child, I think my friend is dead. And we may be in grave danger, quick!" blowing

61

out the candle, gulp, and bullrushing angry lightweight out the door.

The dark street still empty, I locked the door, a fucking expert by now, and croaked a farewell for Perfect Lovelust that didn't exist. Just when we were – oh, he never told me he loved me, oh!

As I pushed my infuriated Marlboro child down the stone steps, he loudly cursed like an old Roman soldier, his pig fucking Mister English guilty of unfair age discrimination, and demanded 500 dirham more for missed cigarette sales plus personal humiliation and injury to his proud Marhueco manhood, which he was shielding with his dirty little hands. I fled.

Of course sleepy Khalid didn't believe my bizarre tale the next day in the tiny deserted TV loft reached by a wood ladder in the seedy cafe near my hotel I'd dragged him to when he'd dropped in early on my sleeplessness, 10 a.m.; he must need dirham.

Leaning over the loft's only scarred mini-table with our cafes au lait untouched, his smug stained, gappy smile, "Por Dios you watch too much strong Marhueco TV, my most delicate foreign wife."

Giggling, shaking my arm, "But now you tell faithful husband Khalid the everything you *really* do with big cock putito (little male whore) cigarette boy, how he fuck Mrs. English ass, my most young camel-stud seducing wife."

My arm jerked away, fist trembling in his salacious face, "Oh shit in your ear Khalid and shit up your mother's cunt, too!" Why did I have such stupid friends? Except for –

Thank god they didn't let Khalid up in my room at my respectable hotel or he'd be living there, and I'd have to move.

Patient explanation attempt, "I was really crazy once, you fucking cretin! I know the difference, like acid, stupid!

As cheerleader captain at Saliva High, I was the guide for all the other cheerleaders tripping on acid. It was OK for football games, outside, dark, lots of space, but for basketball, oh, in those crackerbox gyms with crowds screaming and crying — one double-overtime we lost three cheerleaders to freakouts, and our friends were all throwing their downers at us from the bleachers."

Sarcastic eyebrow lift, "Only once crazy, my most hysterical future ex-wife? Por Dios maybe only once enough for you pues locochón."

Don't call me that oh! Breathe breathe, simmer down for Abdullah, my Scarlet Abdullah, did he ever really exist? Yes, feeling coming back — his slim jamming still warming my ass. I came back, cleared my throat and acted sweet Marhueco, garlanding the sucker with jokey bouquet smiles. "Oh Khalid, you know I was only kidding, I'm just a little upset this morning over what I thought I saw."

Maybe Khalid was right? No, the scarlet was too real, breathe.

My lying español hand soothing his angry stiff arm, "You know you're the very special one whom I chose here to be my only Tangerino tourist guide husband sitting in this godforsaken deserted loft across from me. Uh, oh Khalid, you're so much stronger and more intelligent than those other stupid putos that come up to me on Le Boulevard with their absurd come-ons, like, 'Welcome to Morocco, what do you want, I take you to my brother's shop, no buy only look Por Dios!' "

If only life was as simple as Khalid. He settled back on his little stool, comfortably smug again, his hand on my hand on his arm, tickling it, yes I had feeling back, gracias goddesses. Where was King Hassan II? A quick glance around failed to reveal his photograph — he must be downstairs, he's always somewhere.

La mierda más bonita en español, "Khalid, my most compassionate brother-husband, I feel so close to you now

63

after all our delightful trysts in such unique places a simple tourist could never find by himself. No no, only with such a knowledgeable Tangerino tourist guide, who is more like a brother, no, a husband, no I said that – more, more like myself!" ("¡como mi mismo!")

My hands stroking Khalid above the waist, "Come on, Khalid, my most logical, rational husband, you know I'm a sane Americano, sound businessman, hotel has my travelers checks." Khalid briskly petted back.

"I mean, you know, I'm so together I even rotate my underwear!"

Petting stopped: "You do what in your underwear?"

Obviously wrong example. In español muy claro, "Uh, you know, my highly scientific husband, I read in the *Readers Digest* on the shitter once that advanced Americano Consumer Research Science has conclusively proved that fabric things, such as clothes, sheets and towels, have longer lives if they're periodically rested. So you should always put your clean underwear on the bottom to rotate its use, like tires you know; your mother probably does yours."

Angry hands off, "I don't know what 'tires' means in Mexicano slang, but Por Dios you're not going to rotate your any weird everythings in Honest Khalid's underwear hah! You go back to your putito cigarette boy, his tires big enough for your clunky Americano underwear? And you leave my mother's strict Muslim underwear out of this Por Dios if you want to keep your eye, my too many acid trips wife!"

His disgusted tongue clucked at my shock, then philosophically, "You rich Englishes very nice, but so perverted Por Dios – "

"Goddamn it, Khalid!" So angry I cried again, more for me than Scarlet Abdullah. He was lucky, he was probably dead, I was stuck here with –

Murmuring Khalid sympathetic, scooting his tiny stool

64

next to mine, really holding me in strong, caring arms. Yes at last, the first time since the scarlet − Marlboro boy's brief bumping for dirham didn't count.

Pecking my head and face, tender mumbles, "Oh no no, my newest wife, you do too much in Marhuecos, all poor Khalid's fault Por Dios, make you do too crazy things like la coche and the wall. No no, my sweetest gringita Mexicano, we take little vacation now, alone together now. To the beach at Asilah, very close, small town, Roman ruins for you, quiet love on beach just you and me Por Dios!"

Serious tonguing earwork now − oh well, our tiny loft deserted, not even the King watching my feeling come back. "And you not pay for me, no no, fuckybuddy Khalid go as real brother Por Dios."

Brothers never pay, much less fuckybuddies. But Abdullah was at stake, so I retied myself to Khalid's stake and lit the kindling with soft kisses on his pretty brown face; breathy like Marilyn, "Oh Khalid! That sounds like such fun por dios, my most generous benefactor, yes, we go there of course! But first, just to fix my poor messy brain, so I can feel really relaxed and open and yes! generous there − " Khalid's embrace tightened, pressing his sillybone upright against my black Levi's.

Yes, I was dressed for serious biz today, even wearing old jogging shoes for hasty escapes − or revenge pursuits, my own little Bloody Kansas Jihad (holy war) for Abdullah's precious scarlet; spurned flipflops pouting in the dark under the bed at the hotel.

Routinely working my thigh against uninteresting stubby stiffy rocking his stool, thank goddesses for thick insensitive Levi's. But hot young Khalid groaned at anything and agreed before I suggested it: just dropping by Abdullah's for a minute to clear my silly feminine Americano mind − I still had his key in my pocket but I wanted Khalid along to protect and comfort(?) me. Although my trusty Swiss Army knife was in my pocket

65

too, naturally with the handy roach clip tweezers missing
– I'd corkscrew 'em to death!

Impatiently, I waited for Khalid to finish his morning
TV, in which I indulged only lightly for today must be
together for once. We finally scrambled down the steep
short ladder from the loft to pay another toothless grinny
low cafe owner. He assured us in español that the TV
business would surely pick up in the late afternoon when
his clientele awoke.

Walking Khalid, actually Khalid walking me, fast but
calmly through light midmorning traffic, Tanger a night
town, down a few slanting blocks to the Grand Souk's
drowsy daytime market, then up to Abdullah's whatever;
he was probably exiled or dead, we'd never again –

Whoops, the agile Marlboro boy on the outer fringe
of the round Grand Souk plaza, his scuffed joggers
harassing the few pedestrians ignoring him. He sure
worked long hours, poor kid. But I tugged on Khalid to
give the fierce Marlboro mini-man a wide berth. Laughing
Khalid dragged me straight towards the shabby little
hawker who was waving and shouting at us in Arabic.

"Hah, I know that puto, he on street for years, he do
anything for dirham Por Dios – has dead father too many
brothers and sisters, dumb assholes breed like rats!"

The tough little cigarette guy rushed smiling up at my
face, "Bonjour Monsieur," pumping my hand with baby
fingers that – . We all slapped our chests, "L'bas."

Khalid avuncular, "My strong Marhueco youth, I hear
you took 100 dirham from my dearest amigo Californiano
last night without rotating his tired underwear. You did
not fulfill his weird English tastes; we must please the
tourists here Por Dios!"

Gasping, I grabbed Khalid as the boy grabbed me; in
his confident low imploring español, "Oh I put my
everything in your underwear today, Mister English, very
quiet and calm in your not sick friend's room. I want to

66

love you cool Americano man, we have such fun last night!" The boy's outsized dirham lust poked my black Levi's with Khalid gripping my other side.

Goddesses help me, poor Abdullah! as my Madonna mind and body by Marlon sumo'ed out of Grand Souk lust sandwich prontito! (very fast!) With my sweet but close-mouthed smile — all those toothy tourist grins were starting to hurt – from a safe distance, "It's such an honor and pleasant surprise seeing you here again so soon, young man. How about I buy a pack of Marlboros? One for my friend here too. And one to go. Beautiful morning, no?" handkerchiefing my August face walk-sweat, 11 a.m. and it must be fucking 80° already. Mosquito bites on face, legs, and feet beginning to torment; funny, I'd forgotten all about them in last night's perfect lovelust oh. Better not to feel.

The boy nodded his messed touseled hair with blond-rust casts in the daylight. Khalid was impressed as the wee lad tucked his disproportionate tool under his baggy jacket for future sale. Tight slit eyes as he shook three packs out of his commodious jacket sleeve, then stuck my 50 dirham bill in his shabby pants without offering me my 5 dirham change.

"So how are your socks today?" (Oh no, wrong subject!)

Marlboro poster boy quick to anguish: "Oh poor socks very empty today, my Mister Americano," pulling up his grubby pants legs too far to reveal apparently empty socks that had been slept in too many nights. And hairless scrawny white birdlegs; he definitely looked better by crazed candlelight.

Tough, "But you give me my 700 dirham right now and I not tell anyone about kinky smashed banana Mister English!"

Khalid was dependably rough, but too loud as usual, so I stepped back as he shook the defiant cigarette boy.

They argued in Arabic, then the boy submitted, trailing us as we walked away, the lilt back in his gutter español, "Hey amigo Americano, buy a carton, three or four, have for future! See you tonight, Big Mister Think He Can Hurt Me Man, Hah!"

Laughing Khalid led relieved me through a white stucco keystone arch into the aged Medina's closed life, life closed? Up curving Roman-soldierless steep steps, to there. He took the key from me but the door was bolted from the inside — we could hear faint rock n roll; this was the dangerous part.

Deep breathing, I rapped decisively on fate's door as Khalid shouted bossy instructions in Arabic. The bolt slid and the door opened to a pretty young woman's face. Expressionless, she motioned us inside.

Khalid's laugh helloed bright-candled Abdullah, lying perfectly there in his flowered trow, smiling on his no-killum bed, his black belly hair curling over wide white bandages.

As the bolt shot closed, I fled to my perfect lovelust with his pack of Marlboros outstretched — and fucking fainted into Khalid's strong, laughing arms.

Joy to the Cosmos! I awoke, eyelids fluttering, on a white sheet squeezed beside my Perfect Abdullah, Alive! Now we could continue laughing at life's impossible problems together, from our convalescent bed.

I was all over him, but gently with patting hands and soft teary kisses, evoking painful groans from him. His large hands were still so strong, rudely pushing me off the narrow bed onto the floor. I heard coarse, chorused laughter – what was this perfect lovelust shit anyway? All that suffering, and he wasn't even dead. I considered fainting again for his sympathy, but I was already lying crushed on the hard killumed floor, how would he even know? Or care?

So I pretended to be A Real Man, jumped up and shook his hand solemnly, making his eyes twinkle dull gold as we tapped our chests, "L'bas."

Abdullah's slow, weak smile-voice, "Thank you for helping me, mister angel man. I guess you really do care about me, and now I owe you one."

Only another lifetime of perfect lovelust, you fucking jerk. "Oh shucks, 'tweren't nothin."

Sitting on the edge of the bed, not touching my husband, "What do you mean, help you? I couldn't do anything and then you weren't even here!"

Khalid interrupted of course in fast, jocular Arabic about the long dong Marlboro slutboy, with obscene gestures and many squalid lies, judging from the laughter – pained from cruel suffering Abdullah and polite from his pretty young lady friend. She had joined Khalid on low stools at the end of the bed, candlelight shadowing their faces.

Was she the French-Arabic teacher from good family who really saved his life? She had him now for sure, gulp, so dignified but friendly in a shiny green jellaba, simple gold jewelry and sandals, black hair with light fluff, sharp intelligent nose, probably wore contacts – so calm and together she didn't stand a chance in hell with a puto loco like Abdullah! Or was I projecting again?

Quick check of Madonna, Marlon, even blond surfhunks and airbrushed playgirls for clues, advice, omens. Nada nothing, good, stay up there on peeling flickering wall where you belonged. But thanks for chasing me outta here last night, before, what?

Ah, intense, incomprehensible Arabic was explaining all, Khalid undoubtedly getting a much richer version of last night's events than I'd ever hear. "Goddamn it, hablen Mexicano por favor, stop abusing delicate foreigner suffering extreme culture shocks!"

Abdullah gently pulled me down beside him, our heads

propped on pillows, his long caring hand on my thigh, damned Levi's. I kicked off worthless jogging shoes, sorry I mistrusted you, dear flipflops; I knew they could hear me now that we were all alive again.

Soft weak español, "I'll let Sueád tell you, locochón. It still hurts when I talk, breathe, anything."

Broad Kansaño outrage, "This boy's in pain! Aren't there any drugs in this fuckin' country?!"

Our predictable laughter subsided into poor Abdullah's soft groans from his untouched dark chest with perfect black curls I wanted to brunch on. When did I eat last, anyway?

Low, pained, "Shut up locochón — you want to hurt me more?"

Quiet passion squeezing his hand lifeless on my thigh, "What do you mean, I helped you? You always say all I do is talk."

Khalid cocky, "I tell you Abdullah too young, not real man like strong Khalid, 25, experienced, Por Dios I rotate your tires forever!" his legs apart on his stool, crotch crunching, the young woman smiling at uncomfortable me.

Abdullah squeezed my hand back, low, "No, you put the clothes and books on me, helped keep the blood in me, says my friend there, meet Sueád."

Smiling familarly by now, introductions sometimes took awhile here, she rose and offered me her left hand to shake which surprised me. For the sensible old Arab custom was to eat with your right, shit with your left. But they say young Arabs don't always follow this practice anymore, and Sueád certainly seemed a modern Arab woman.

So we shook left hands, she explaining in calm cultured, educated español that she'd hurt her right arm in a motorcycle accident recently. Huh?

Smiling sweetly at Sueád, nervous español rattling, "Oh I know just what you mean, Sueád! Too many fucked-up knees and elbows — I finally had to sell my dear old

70

battered bike when all the Americano health insurance companies threatened to declare bankruptcy," discovering I was still pumping her hand, quickly letting it drop to more jolly gyrations from Khalid.

Sueád sat back down on her stool, her brown face pure in the candlelight, calm low español casi perfecto, "You see, last night I was coming up here to see Abdullah when I saw you trying to lock his door. I could tell you were extemely agitated, especially when you grabbed that poor cat and tried to kiss it. It had to scratch you to get away."

Huh? I thought those were kinda long mosquito bites on my face that Khalid had teased me about this morning. Quick hands to my face, we'd have to get some wall mirrors in here, strategically placed, when I became aware of their mirth stirred again, even suffering Abdullah hack-laughing.

Sueád continued cheerfully, "So I stood in a dark doorway until you ran by, my, your plastic beach sandals sounded like gunshots on the steps!"

"I was shooting Roman soldiers in self-defense!"

Arched bitch eyebrow, "So that's why you screamed."

Amused Khalid mopping his face, leaning off his stool, "Por Dios! I always tell you wear real shoe, but no no, you never listen to your Khalid till he dead, you disgrace me falling off that baby wall – "

Flaring, "Shut the fuck up, Khalid!"

After getting the last laugh with a world-weary sighing shrug in Italiabic, Khalid shut up, leaned back, and resumed playing with himself.

Encouraging smile for real life campfire story teller, "And what did you do then, Sueád?"

Chuckling, "Well, the way you were behaving made me wonder what strange act Abdullah had committed this time," her dark eyes narrowed at him. He removed his hand from mine on my thigh, intertwining his fingers on his chest – long fingers that had been sizzling rough

71

sensitive everywhere on, in me, only a lifetime ago, now absently toying with his lonely chest hairs.

Sueád's eyes black serious in mine, "I have a key, and well, I just couldn't believe it. I can't say I was particularly surprised, but —"

Fast turn to Abdullah, "It was that guy you were muttering with at your Marlboro stand yesterday!"

Sueád's cold español jerked my head around: "Number one: Don't be ridiculous; that's not how these things are done. And number two: Don't even speculate in your own mind about a thing that cannot concern a foreign tourist. Moroccans not like other people, they kill you."

Stunned, "Oh, yeah, I know, uh, Khalid's told me all about it, uh, I'll be good, I promise!"

Her friendly smile back, "Good. Anyway, even though I'm a nursing student, it's still a terrible shock, especially when it's someone you know, a friend, seeing him lying there a bloody mess with the clothes and books on him, and covered up with a blanket and the candle on to help with the shock. I admired your courage then."

Oh, should I fall in worship love on her sparkling gold sandals? Instead, "Oh, so you're not the literature teacher from good family!"

Khalid back, "Oh her, hah! Abdullah's ghost fiancee — you know how gay boy always lie to family about their many girl friend!"

It cost Abdullah a mighty groan to hurl his round metal kif box, but the clunk it made on howling Khalid's head satisfied all. Laughing Khalid naturally began preparing a pipe from it.

"But, but where did you take him, Sueád? I couldn't have been gone more than a few minutes?"

"About 15," checking her sturdy nurse's watch. "I feared you would find your way back up here after I saw how you'd fixed up Abdullah, and we don't even know you. So I quickly wrapped his wounds with a clean shirt and towel and cleaned up the mess. When I heard your beach sandal racket coming up the steps, I quickly took our patient there, on a little vacation, there!" pointing at our bed.

"But–but I sat on this bed, the cigarette boy is my witness," ignoring Khalid's boring obscene jests in Arabic.

Abdullah's love hand patted my thigh — I had known him more lifetimes than you, bitch! Weak but mocking love, "You didn't open it up, look underneath. Platform beds very convenient for storage, mister not think of everything, man."

Oh — . Thank goddesses I hadn't gotten carried away with Marlboro nymphoboy, they knew everything, they'd been right under us. They?

"Did you fit in there too, Sueád?"

Giggling, eyes alive, "It was a tight squeeze, but I kept Abdullah quiet," sharply rebuking Khalid's smartass Arabic crack.

Khalid bogarted the bark stick pipe I thought I'd never suck on again. Sueád took ladylike tokes like mine, but I took more, time to celebrate perfect lovelust's survival!

Suddenly, paranoid hands shaking my love carefully, "Uh, Abdullah, shouldn't we be just a little concerned about something like that, like happening again, like here?"

Abdullah's kif-strenghtened laugh made me laugh too. "I think they got the message. My blind Homer-raping fishing family, remember, locochón?" his green gold eyes alive again, thank you Jesus, I mean Mohammed, I mean kif, I mean me, I mean us, I mean everything.

I woke up, "Oh yeah. Mother-raping fisherfolks, so what?"

Tourist guide Khalid, "That means mister shafra (curved Berber knife) is swimming to Gibraltar right now, on the bottom! After a good Marhueco tongue-twisting," they laughed merrily, then Abdullah cough-moaned some more.

"But, but – "

73

Authoritative nurse's tones, "Let's just say that since Abdullah insists on staying here, his family has people out there," indicating the menacing Medina beyond the heavy bolted doors.

"My, my, I'm impressed — pretty good for a humble pirate family. Pirates! Smugglers! Abdullah's the *real* Marlboro Man!"

Heavy laughter, except for Sueád, who look pained-perplexed at Abdullah — the way my mother used to look at my dad, when as a pre-schooler I'd throw off all my clothes and run on the tops of the furniture shrieking gleefully above the hilarious heads of the company — farmers are earthy and I was spoiled.

Sincerely beguiling, "Oh Abdullah, you just said I saved your life and everything. Oh please, sweetie, you know I'm looking for an interesting job here, please could I be a smuggler with your family? I mean just an apprentice smuggler of course, maybe part-time till I learn the ropes. Wouldn't have to start me off at much — do they pay commission or what? Oh please, please Abdullah — I always rooted for the Barbary Pirates in my Saliva history classes!"

But brave pirate son Abdullah was caught up in his own anguished laugh-hacking battle, finally recovering sufficiently to push me off the bed onto my friend, the floor, again.

Low, angry, "I told you not to make me laugh. You go now, locochón, you agitate me too much, I need rest."

Fuck fucked-up lovelust! I knew it was just a myth, but so much fun while it lasted — everything so new, funny, pure, light.

But now back to blubbering youngest Saliva child, standing there being lied to and left behind again. "But–but Abdullah! You know I really care for you and want to take care of you and I don't have a job, I have time — and we've even got real bandages now," trailing my fingers where snowy white adhesive lost itself in black belly hairs overlapping it; the tingle went straight to my crotch and Abdullah winced in pain.

Chuckling to rewind spaghetti mind, yes! "Hey Abdullah, in a day or two when you're feeling better, you need to get away from all this Medina shafra madness. What do you say we take a real vacation, like a little trip down to Asilah for a few days, a couple of weeks – the beach, so peaceful they say, just you and me – "

Khalid's roar hurt my ears, "Hey! Por Dios that's where we're going alone together! Honest Khalid pay the everything, don't you remember anything? Too much fuckin' acid putón!"

Shocked, "Oh! I forgot, I'm sorry, Khalid."

Orator Khalid on feet, shaking his fist at noble Abdullah, "That worthless faggot puto can't do anything for your tires now anyway, Por Dios you need real man Khalid!" gyrating his pathetic bulge at me.

Pained to extreme patience, "Oh please Khalid, don't be such a clown, it's against the law for you to think. Or to be the least bit sensitive in this medical emergency we're trying to deal with rationally – "

I heard rather than felt Khalid's fist crunching my right eye. From far away in the darkness, oh dear, had we knocked the candle over? I heard emergency nurse screams and fought rough hands prying me off security rock Abdullah, who was writhing in painful Frenchabic cough curses.

Then banging on door and blinding daylight shooting excruciatingly into what had been my eye. Swarthy and very firm smuggling security men escorted abashed Khalid and me down curving stone steps. Where were those jackoff Roman soldiers when I needed them? Probably off at the glory holes.

They left us with muttered Arabic warnings under the arch to the Grand Souk. I angrily shoved Marlboro pest away who was jumping to kiss "for comfort and heal" my bleeding closed eye held gingerly under my handkerchief and pissed but apologetic Khalid's purple Americano bandana.

Cigarette boy's last defiant shouts, "I find who do this to you and kill fucking puto who can't take his punishment from Sweet Mister English!"

There will be no trip to Asilah; I will not be waiting in my hotel at sadistic Khalid's appointed time tomorrow. No no, I shall sail my Barbary Pirate ship back to the mysterious Medina – for as goons were dragging me dazed through his door, I saw coy Abdullah's gold glitter green winks at me, Por Dios – Perfect Love Lust Lives!

MR. DAWSON AS LIZ TAYLOR

"Shitfuckcock, Khalid! I can't go to a job interview with this stupid bandage on my eye and fucking cat scratch fever all over my face!"

Mi español muy dramático, mugging in the solid band of mirrors around the respectable Boulevard Pasteur cafe – cloth tablecloths, even, and the only TV the one on the wall with a large color soccer game en español. At 9:30 a.m.? Maybe tape delay, maybe from Tierra del Fuego, who knew?

Or cared that handsome young Khalid's face was bright and clean-shaven today, but oh so weathered with concern. In his pobre español, muy humilde, "I'm so sorry my only wife that I'm a too strong man Por Dios, hit you too mightily yesterday."

Whirling from my mirror mourning, my surviving steel blue eye drilled him; he nervous chuckled, then smiled seriously, "But even you know you can't say those things to a proud Marhueco man Por Dios!"

As my drill blazed him, Khalid chuckled to sorrowful, gingerly holding up his slightly swollen, vaguely pinkish-brown right fist, voice hurt, "You injured me too, my strongest wife."

Disgusted snort, "If we were in America, you'd be in jail!"

Proud chin jut, "In Marhuecos, you're lucky to still be alive, my canniest wife."

Staring down at the green tablecloth under its shiny glass cover, sighing, "Oh just fuck it ese and fuck you too." My head raised ominously, firm eye, "But let me warn you, my most disgusting ex-husband, once victim twice fool. Comprendez vous?"

Taking my hand lovingly, triumphant voice, "¡Simón locochón!" (Maybe teaching him more romantic Mexicano might civilize him.)

I glanced around, guessed it was okay to hold hands here; after all, our couple was half Arab and half locochón. Our uninterested fellow breakfasters, reading newspapers or softly chatting in Arabic, mostly watching the soccer game, assumed routinely I supposed that nicotine-stained, gaptoothed puto was fleecing the faggot tourist for all he was worth and beating him up in the bargain. They were half right.

The King was here of course, prominently photo-displayed, young in a white military uniform, he took many guises. Squirming painfully on my comfortable green padded chair, "Oh I just can't believe that fucking export company director cut short his trip to Nueva York and is back in fucking Tanger already. Westerners have no sense of time – "

Bright black-eyed Khalid was too stupid to field my slow rolling satire, but he had the cunning to be waiting early this morning, 9 a.m., when flipflopping Marhueco rookie on the DL (disabled list) crept down the worn marble staircase of my hotel to flee from yesterday's attacker whom I didn't even like too much of the time (even if Khalid had been foolishly provoked by my dumb lovelust for now imperfect, too-coy Abdullah).

My pain-swollen purple eye had made me reflect on more than the mirror in my hotel room on heavy soap-opera TV, then delayed adolescent sobbing for eternity in hot shower tragedy and joy therapy.

This morning I was off the mental DL and pissed at the world. "So then this jackoff, Dawson y Dawson Exports his name, calls my hotel this morning at 8 a.m.! He must be some kind of a nut, and left a message, for the desk has orders not to put any calls through before 11, that he liked my resume bullshit and to come to his office this afternoon! Looking like I been through the Tanger meatgrinder – " posing tragically in the mirrors again: white gauze taped

78

over my right eye, plus thin red scablines on cheek and nose from the unfortunate liaison with the cat. In fact, I could see four pitiful me's in the mirror across the six tables–wide cafe.

Khalid patiently waiting for his breakfast. "It's only one eye, my loudest-voiced wife, and Sueád fixed it very well for you. Por Dios you look so beautiful today, my everyday wife," mocking gap smile.

Low, rapidly, "Sueád was there for only a few minutes and she nursed, I mean doctored, me down in the lobby. All she said was she and Abdullah weren't really lovers and all his friends have keys to his humble cave."

My sole eye fixed suspiciously on Khalid's countenance to decipher his reaction to Sueád's story, probably another helping of Tangerino camelshit. Khalid only smiled sweetly.

Disgusted, "So how the fuck do you know already about her coming there? It was only last night – "

Proud, "Tanger small town, I live here all my life, know everybody, everything Por Dios! Now, forgiven Khalid would like to try some of those powerful downers Sueád gave you."

"Huh? How do you know that – god, this is worse than Saliva! And they're pain medication and it's disgusting that you ask me for one – though I guess you were responsible for them, you, you – " They were affecting me already.

Our bickering was broken up by an amiable new waiter in black pants and white shirt with the top two buttons wisely unbuttoned, let that curly black chest hair breathe! Almost all the men were attractive and friendly in Morocco, but could horny blue-eyed devil adjust to bruised paradise?

The waiter set down my regular, "The American Breakfast," a scalding glass of cafe au lait on a silver saucer, a hunk of cold white cheese between two buttery slices of toasted French bread (cholesterol calms the nerves) neatly cut into three pieces for easy eating, while

79

watching the A's pitching fall apart every morning in my *International Herald Tribune*, Twins' year. Khalid smacked down five gooey French-Moroccan pastries and two cafe au lait.

The sweet smelling, delicious (Tangerino food usually is) breakfast raised my blood sugar and enlivened my complaining. "And I suppose I'll have to wear long goddamn pants and a real shirt — fuck the tie."

As Khalid snorted his pastry, "And another thing, Khalid my almost friend, I intend to visit Abdullah's sick bed today. Alone by myself!" ("¡Solamente por mi mimísimo!") Profoundly, "We got a lot to talk about, him and me."

Khalid looked better with his mouth full of whipped cream; I pretended it was la rica leche mía. Spitting my whipped cream cum back at me, "Hah! I know you Por Dios you think you fix everything with your fancy talktalk. But you talk too much crazy shit and change your words too much."

Mohammed the Pope: "You forget, my frivolous wife, that La Palabra Es Siempre (always) La Palabra, for a *real* man Por Dios!"

Angrily attacking my cheese toast with my Saliva orthodontured pearls, "Oh yeah, Mighty Marlboro Man, remember I'm just a fucking wife, good Arab woman spends life stooped! And quit saying fucking 'Por Dios' all the time, that shit's driving me crazy, even on Sueád's powerful downs you'll never touch!"

This latest little outburst caused a couple of middle aged men at the next table to raise solemn black eyes at me over their Moroccan newspapers – how could they read that shit, backwards even! I was glad I was illiterate, for night neon signs in Arabic became beautiful art instead of mere information — sweeping long lines and curls glowing, with diacritical marks bright circles, slashes, or diamonds of light.

The men back to their newspapers, frank one-eyed

stare, low, "Khalid, my very new friend, I think we need a little vacation from each other."

Khalid nonchalantly licking raspberry jam, the scarlet of Abdullah's belly wounds, off his suddenly blurring fingers, "Oh yes, very excellent idea my most devoted wife. I'm busy this afternoon anyway."

Breathing, keeping my dander down in defense of my remaining eye (who says we don't learn?), snake laughter, "Your unique sense of humor delights me, my most clownish husband. But I was thinking more of, like several days vacation, separate, apart from each other you know – until this disgrace heals," pointing to my trump card.

Scarlet fingerlicking ceased, Khalid drew himself straight up in his chair opposite me; I ditto with unfair height advantage from high nutrition culture. His dark eyes wide, decisive, "You know that cannot be. You are my only wife, I love you too much, you are hurting me too much today Por Dios Por Dios Por Dios!"

En low español so not to disgrace ourselves with newspaper men still in backwardsville – though English must be backwards to them. But besides Arabic, everyone studies French left-to-right in Moroccan schools – goddeses, they're bi-linear too! "Khalid, my dearest fuck-up, I have told you oh so many times in our eternal several day relationship, that I want, and intend to have, many men here. Fuck off, man, we're not even going steady. I don't don't don't wanna wanna wanna see you you you every fucking day day day! ¿Comprendes al fin (finally) ese? Por Fucking Dios!"

Khalid's tan playboy face crumpled and fell. We finished breakfast in unnatural silence, concentrating on our food, dry and tasteless now.

Even Khalid knew the power of action over words; soberly he paid the check plus tip, solicitiously walked me across Le Boulevard to my hotel; we solemnly shook hands, French cheek-bussed, tapped our chests. His sad "Bes-

81

lámah" (goodbye in Arabic), my neutral "Incháallah" (if Allah wills), with fingers crossed behind my back.

Well, he was learning Mexicano, maybe I could teach him Dutch treat. Or might that culturally conflict him, like poor Abdullah?

At least it was cool overcast, just muggy this afternoon, the Atlantic blowing the Straits of Gibraltar a white cloud cover over Tanger Bay and its small light city on the hill.

I was picking my way carefully down zigzag streets to the bay, keeping so clean my shiny black shoes, hotel freshly-pressed gray cotton pants, and baggy Guatemalan Huehuetenango huipil (pullover Indian shirt) to my knees, sleeveless with floppy red-patterned collar, worn to add artistic touch plus good luck, Incháallah! my handiest Arabic phrase.

Mr. Dawson, my future employer, I prayed, had left another message at my hotel: to meet him at a restaurant I'd never heard of on Avenue D'Espange (now also called Avenue des FAR to honor the Moroccan armed forces). It was the wide boulevard with four lanes of traffic(!) and parking on both sides, curving Tanger Bay (Buccaneers?).

Stunning to grotesque, shy to brazen young men lounged along the narrow streets down, some offering me various commodities, including themselves, in English, Spanish, French, and Arabic and various combinations of the above – Tanger, International Fun City. But "No gracias, no gracias pues," for today I was a spritely virgin with promises worth keeping.

Reaching the Avenida Whatever, I nervously rechecked my cheap silver Timex. See how unostentatious and practical I am, Mr Dawson? (Think I'll omit my regular Hanes rotation this time.)

Early by nature, I quickly spotted the large but tasteful sign in French and Arabic for the Chateau Poulet (Chicken House?) Restaurant. Good, I'd beat him here, eager beaver first impression. And time to re-rehearse over-rehearsed sincere lies, one more time.

I mumbled eloquently to myself, "Ahem − frankly, Mr. Dawson, it's highly embarrassing for me to come to my job interview looking like I've just been through the Tanger Meatgrinder, heh-heh," pause for laugh. "And naturally, no one ever believes the simple truth behind anyone's probably perfectly innocent eye injury," ignoring scratched face. Pause for positive reinforcement and possibly Mr. Dawson's own innocent black eye anecdote.

"But I'll be darned, Mr. Dawson, if I didn't slip on that wet floor in my hotel room, and bang my damn eye on the douche–urinal, and scratch my poor cheek and nose on the douche faucet," praying that mildly salacious, vaguely bisexual douche–urinal reference might distract puritanical 8 a.m. Mr. Dawson from my pathetic lies regardless of his sexual persuasion.

I breathed the two steps up to a spacious patio in front of the ritzy-titsy two-story restaurant. I looked around approvingly at the smart black and white metal tables and chairs with large yellow beach umbrellas. The patio was glass-walled to protect diners from sometimes stiff bay winds, none today.

Only the railroad tracks and a string of clubs and restaurants separated me from the wide sand beach so clean you could walk across it barefoot without bloodying your feet (oh, Abdullah!). I wanted to be running across brown sand, deep breathing nude, plunging into brace-chilling ancient Mediterranean waves via blip of Tanger Bay, where I longed to be splashing to the center of my universe with dark fuckbuddies flashing white laughter and sightly boned bikinis.

Instead of fucking standing here handkerchiefing collected humidity in the chic Chicken Chateau my ass, plastering down sweaty hair with hands (fuck! shoulda got a haircut), fingering fresh eye bandage throbbing lightly, picking off a couple of last minute nose scabs, breathing to get sad show on the road, turning myself in again, into what and for whom? But no money no honey, honeys, I know I know I know.

A solitary diner at the only occupied table on the patio – late afternoon siesta time for toditos (all) Los Tangerinos, except el putón Señor Dawson, surely a slave driving pre-vert. If he expected me to get up at 6:30 in the morning to be late to work at 8, he had a camel up his ass. Hmmm, haven't seen one fucking real camel here – maybe in the zoo? Though I could probably buy one from the long dong Marlboro boy.

Why was the occupant of the sole occupied table interrupting my pleasant Sueád-medicated siesta musings? Standing, waving, even calling me by name. Some old Catholic aunt from Eastern Kansas who worshipped Paul Harvey?

Too loud, "Hey! Over here – I'm Dawson!"

She looked like Liz Taylor gone frowsy housewife.

Blinking, feets moving, "Uh, uh, Mr. Dawson?"

Housewife Liz laughed raucously (a good sign). "That's my husband, we're divorced kinda, he runs the New York operation. These damned hotels here never get messages straight no matter what lingo you use with the bastards!" (Oh good, she cussed!)

We shared long weary laughter over the woes of underdevelopment while still pumping hands, honorable Midwestern tradition.

"Sit down, let me get a good look at you," deep throaty voice (neat!).

I breathe-composed myself next to her at the round white table, settling comfortably on my black plastic seat cushion, stretching my legs under the table, carefully together. We smile-studied each other, she an older natural beauty, humorously unconcerned about her flimsy flowered housedress, salt and pepper curls awry. Her only make-up was her perfect pink complexion — I wanted to pinch her apple cheeks like my dead grandmother's, I mean when she was alive — I'd better listen!

"— so you'll excuse my appearance," not bothering with the affectation of patting her hair as she said it. "But as you know, I just got back in town last night, early and unexpected. So of course," her cynical laughter sunshine, "the orders were a *little* behind. So I've been straw boss and slave in the shipping department, last night and since the crack of dawn today. Not that we're short-handed, just that our hands are a little short on punctuality and ambition."

We clucked our tongues and shook our heads like two mad dog Brits in the Raj, Ms. Dawson's violet-grey Liz eyes out to lunch.

Yes! One of those unstructured, conversation-type job interviews with nice neurotic open older woman — ¡Simón! Friendly collie pup wagging my tongue, "Oh I know just what you mean, Ms. Dawson, about the sad lack of ambition in the world today. I'm an old hard working Kansas farmboy myself!"

Her sharp now violet eyes curious on my face. Oh fuck! My lines! Quick to Neil Diamondsap, "Very frankly, Ms. Dawson, I must apologize to you for my, uh, temporary appearance today. It's so embarrassing to come to a job interview looking like I've been ravished by the Barbary Pirates, heh-heh — "

Her full, deep-pink lips pursed sympathetically, her voice husky soft, "Oh yes, you poor boy. I know all about it, your hotel told me they're so concerned about you."

Gulp! Keep face together, "Oh. They did? They are?"

"Yes." She lit a black market Marlboro, I politely but non-condemningly declined one; fighting the shakes but can't do moving–parts things right now.

Desperate lite, "Well, heh-heh, that was really something. What do you think of it, uh, now?" Oh goddesses,

85

you know I always supported Liz! Even when I saw those old pathetic photos Debbie posed for with the safety pins in her flannel shirt, Eddie wasn't worth it, hell of a crooner though.

Exhaling delicious Marlboro smoke in my face that I surreptitiously deep breathed, Ms. Dawson shrugged her broad flowered shoulders, "I don't know. Just be more careful getting out of the shower in those cheap hotels, I guess."

¡Oh mil besos diosas! (A thousand kisses, goddesses!) And for the hotel desk clerk, too, obviously skilled in obtaining large tips. But that must be an over-used lie, must invent a new one − later.

Giddy, "Oh yes yes! You're so right Ms. Dawson, if I may call you that!"

Short, "That's my damn handle." Leaning confidentially until our bodies touched, her plump jeweled white hand on mine (be cool Liz). "But you're smart not to waste your money on expensive lodging here during the high tourist season. In September the prices will all come down and we'll find you a nice but inexpensive apartment. If you take the job."

My body jerking into hers, blurt, "You mean that's it? I got it with no bullshit? That's not fair, I had all these proven lines thunk up!"

Ms. Dawson slapped my hand trembling joy and ejaculated blowsy laughter, rocking her soft Liz body against mine. "You're a funny, cute one. You'll be good with the dealers and customers. They all speak at least market Spanish or English. And I assume you're finding many volunteers here to teach you Arabic and French," widening black bushes around her jeweled violets. I smiled shy agreement.

Returning to her own body, seriously stubbing out her Marlboro, "I liked your resume, my, you've certainly had a lot of jobs." (She should see all the ones I left out!) "So

I called that Guatemalan shop in The City, I know it, I grew up in San Francisco, well, Mountain View actually.... Nice Huehuetenango huipil you're wearing, by the way, even if you did cut the sleeves off," fingering its floppy collar, I a stolid Roman soldier.

"Muchísimas gracias buena Señora Dawsóne," bowing my head to my benefactress. Goddesses Diosas the both of them — my funny wonderful new boss, and Saintly Liz who has done more publicity and fund-raising for AIDS than the putón Republican White House.

Low Liz biz-tones, "Anyway, they raved about you at 'Guatepeor,' funny name for a shop."

Teaching, "The complete name is 'Sale de Guatemala, Entra en Guatepeor,' from bad to worse, a humorous old Spanish idiom."

Impatient toss of silver-black mess, "I know, I know. Uh, they also said you were their best Latin American buyer, plus you did everything in the store cheerfully and well: sell, pack, do phones, help keep the books. I must admit I was impressed, and I don't impress easily. As you'll find out soon enough," her voice suddenly gone hard on me. Oh, slap me, Liz, grind me with your naughty high heel in the Butterfield 8 Motel!

Overly secure, "Well, they *are* my best friends from back in Saliva."

Suspicious, "Saliva?"

"Oh, ha, that's what we called our hometown, Salina – Kansas. Like Tapuke-a, Topeka you know."

My, she had a hearty laugh. "I do now."

Then she probed my good eye with hers. Ah, homefield advantage, for I lied best while sincerely meditating in my victim's eyes. "Well, my bright young Saliva man, we'll soon find out what you can do. I'm going to start you out downstairs in shipping and receiving so you can learn the product and our procedures. Thirty-five hours a week, Monday through Friday, starting pay is 6,000 dirham a month, about 660 bucks, good starting pay here, but with all your experience – . We pay health insurance and full dental, your basic rights as a human being. What shift would you like to work?"

Reeling but still sane, "Afternoons and evenings por favor! I'm still rebelling in my old age against my crack-o-dawn Norman Rockwell farm youth – full of chicken shit and rednecks."

Narrow eyes greying, "I'll bet. You're gay, aren't you?"

"Uh, yes." Innocent wide eye, "I hope that doesn't make any difference."

Her whooping laughter clapped my back, lightning jolted my bad eye, "In this business? In Tanger? You're an innocent comedian, like an ignorant clown. You'll go far here!"

Lusty growl, "I bet you're in pure pig heaven in Tanger, with all these beautiful cheap, thieving boys!"

"Who, me?" Sky-blue shocked in mocking violets, "Well, to tell you the truth, Ms. Dawson, actually I've spent most nights here in my hotel room reading. Or sometimes I go to the cafes, to read outdoors in these pleasant cool but warm Tanger evenings you have here. I joined the American Library, you know, by the interesting old American Legation Museum in that scary old Medina, all tunnels and dead-ends, I get lost in there every time, just like the ghost house at the Saliva County Fair!"

She nodded, impressed, or bored? "The library has 6,000 volumes in English. And lots of books about Morocco and North Africa. I like the fiction best, it tells more, you know, about the people, their feelings and motivations, plus fiction writers describe locales more vividly Por Dios than those boring chingón nonfiction shithouse books like *National Geographic*. They used to piss me off, they'd show tit, but no cock or balls, maybe a little pube once in awhile – "

She was asleep sitting there, poor thing, such a long

day. So I cleared my throat loudly to arouse her for my quiet dramatic summation: "So. I suppose you could just say, Ms. Dawson, that I'm more an escapist, aesthetic Susan Sontag–type person. I'd rather read about it, or see it in a worthwhile film than actually go out and do it — I'll leave that to braver, more adventuresome types than I!" fast modest schoolboy grin.

Fully awake and laughing, impressed, "My dear boy, with a line of Tapuke-a crap like that, you'll live like a king here!" slapping my pouty shoulder, fuck Huehuetenango!

Handkerchiefing madly, "Oh yeah? Well just let me tell you what's happened to me already!"

The Good Queen Liz probably saved my job by interrupting testily, "Where the fuck's that lazy bastard waiter? Can you believe we haven't even been waited on yet?"

Angrily but gracefully rising, no purse; wallet and keys sensibly deep in large pockets of her thin flowered housedress. Friendly, "Come on, I'll show you your new place of employment. It's just a block from here. I'm sure you're not very hungry, you're new here, probably eating all day. And all night too!" lewd pokes with rude hee-haws to my standing ribs. Do It Do It Liz, and if that's what getting up at 8 a.m. does for you, I'll give it a try, next lifetime. Home free in this life, a real employed Tangerino at last!

My Ms. Liz Dawson plump pleased as I smacked a big kiss on her smooth apple cheek as we departed the Chicken House patio uneaten to my new life. Oh now Proud Abdullah would be so proud of his locochón — would he say I love only you forever at last?

MUSTAPHA, ARABIAN STALLION

But that night, less than perfect Abdullah turned disbelieving, then pissed off: "What do you mean you fucked on the packing table your first day at work, you fucking locochón?!"

Slightly squirming on his bed with its new gray and black killum, I renewed my pledge to the whole truth, for without it, perfect lovelust could never be. I quickly handed rude Abdullah the long stick kif pipe with its fragrant red ember; he'd soon be back to his usual mocking laughter.

Patiently correcting as he sucked smoke: "It wasn't on the packing table, it was on the inspection table. And it wasn't my first day at work, my first day is tomorrow. Today I was just being shown around the place by Elizabeth Taylor playing Ms. Dawson of Dawson y Dawson Exports."

Blowing angry perfume in my face, "You mean you fucked with that Mrs. Dawson? You said she was old woman, you going mother-complex bi on me locochón?"

Reassuring Saliva hands on large flat, hardening black nips, playing with their tight curls, in español romántico, "Please, Abdullah, my first and last perfect husbandwife, please listen to your devoted servant's woeful tale, full of personal humiliation and disgrace."

Our bed heads together, lost in his long black ringlets, "You see, Ms. Dawson was just telling me about the boring office bullshit part − but then to show me around the packing and stockroom downstairs, she turned me over to this Mustapha guy who happened to drop by, Incháallah, I mean Hámdullah!" (thanks Allah)

Abdullah set the pipe on the bedside table and turned his poor torn belly wrapped in smaller fresh bandages into mine − we had taken the precaution of removing our clothes – and in his dreamy voice so noble, "Oh good! Tell me an exciting fuck story, I need it, and you're funnier than real TV!"

So I turned away, indulged in a couple of dainty puffs to enliven my story for me, sipped Sidi Ali water, shared a fig with Abdullah's mouth, our tongues winning. Back to soft cock to cock, "Well, to make a short story long – and Abdullah, honey, was he ever long!"

Sincere and perky, Mary Tyler Moore's first day on the job that started tomorrow, I'd tried to follow dull and confusing office procedures rattled off tonelessly by Ms. Dawson. But my mind was still on holiday, already rearranging the simple furniture in my perfect little Medina apartment, with posters of Lovely Liz, that I could rent now – solid citizen of Tanger with job, boy friends, and Moroccans becoming familiar on the street staring at my battered face.

Slumped in her padded black desk chair, frazzled Ms. Dawson droned on, about – invoices again? She'd hassled too many hours today.

A dark white-hooded apparition glided in from the alley street, alighting in the doorway of Dawson y Dawson Exports like he owned the crammed two-desk office, filing cabinet, computer terminal and fax machine, plus god-knew-what in the basement.

"You look too beat, Ms. Dawson, you poor thing," boomed the apparition softly leaning in the doorway too narrow, too short for his giant body lurking under a shiny, white-ribbed jellaba with the hood up, the closet office expanding in his slow low accented English.

Concern furrowed his dark canyoned brow snow-plowing a V to above his nose, a proud brown skijump; his slow pity resounded, "Oh my poor Ms. Dawson, you go home now, work is finish, you go sleep now. I will take care of new guy," flinging his meathand at me, his black

91

hairy tree-trunk arm popping from his jellaba gleaming white as were his well manicured teeth protruding from a softly whinnying, oversized smile. I bet my hardening tongue would fit perfectly between erotic natural gaps of his beautiful horse teeth.

Duty with dignity, "I will show new guy the rest."

The Rest? I tried not to overgape him, peeking over the tops of silly trembling shipping invoices written in near English. Mighty Stallion of Arabia! T.H. Lawrence was right, of course!

Mustapha's massive mahogany face and hands stunning out of his white jellaba vibrating kindness for me, his taut lantern jaw clean-shaven, black patterned dots smooth to his teeth-spitting smile that forced my melting good eye to sweaty hands dropping wrecked invoices.

I groped for my handkerchief as sleep-walking Ms. Dawson shuffled her sensible gray gunboats in disheveled flowered housedress to the grinning apparition glowing in the doorway, his soft brown horse's eyes moistly burning my good one again.

In tired smoker's strained voice, Ms. Dawson addressed my new thoroughbred, patient in the gate. "Yeah, Mustapha, I hired the California one who slipped in the bathroom," turning to me frozen in chair at the desk I prayed would never be mine as I tried to remember not to forget to breathe.

Forced tired smile, "This is Mustapha, uh, he works around here sometimes."

Liz sighing housewife fed up with it all, "I'm sorry but I've been dead on my feet since 6 a.m. this morning. Es la hora for casa y vino. See you tomorrow afternoon, say two-ish, and we'll go over this silly office shit again. I don't even remember what I showed you." (me neither, Liz honey)

Turning back to Mustapha who smiled superiorly(?) at the cold(?) edge in her voice, "I showed him in here,

92

Mustapha. If before you leave you could just run him through the downstairs. Don't bother with procedures, just a quick look. He'll have plenty of time later to learn the work down there."

Brown and pink horse lips spread wide and whinnied gleefully, I swear!

Biz Liz rote, "Everybody's gone home now, we finally finished the fucking orders. The night watchman will be by soon to lock up."

Ms. Dawson determinedly pushed her graceful heft past the pawing steed, scarcely touching his pulsating white jellaba filling the doorway as she disappeared onto the street.

A fit of sanity sprang me to the door through the white lightning ghost, "Hey! Thanks so much again, you're so kind, Ms. Dawson! I love my job already, you're all so nice here, and now I get to live here – Buenos Días El Tanger, Hasta Luego La Saliva, Pues!"

Collective silly laughter revived Liz's nonchalant bounce in her flowered dance frock up the dirty little street to casa.

But perilous laughter waves had tossed me into hairy horse arms, actually Mustapha's thick left foreleg propped against the door jamb. The dark bay foreleg tightened around me as he closed and locked the door with his other. His cloven hooves engulfed my shoulder going hard – and such chocolate cloves he had – gross fat all the way down their black hairy lengths to square nubby tips: everybody knows what that means. And short clipped nails the size of American quarters, the better to rub my erect shoulder now thrusting against them.

We faced each other (my face, his chest), Mustapha's hot bulk enveloping, weakening me, his electric horse prod vibrating his jellaba and fatally wrinkling my job interview pants.

Tender loving by a giant is highly theraputic, giving the illusion, thus the experience, of strength and security

for a minute. Or for a millenia, I prayed up into Mustapha's dark horse eyes, gentling as he soft-nuzzled me, "Hi,
Frisco Boy, I'm your Mustapha – Long Beach State, class
of '81!"

I next remember the glare and heat of a close room
hung solidly around with bright killums of many colors and
in shiny stacks on the worn carpeted packing room floor.
The gentle brown giant lifted me to sit on a high wide
table, my purebred so many hands high that his standing
jellaba'ed crotch pressed between my thighs that he'd
spread with his strong hind legs. Warmest, fuzziest
forelegs enraptured me around and around, from wet
joyface to barely sitting, twitching ass.
He flirted his sausage-tasting tongue with mine, then
moved his dripping meatloaf to flit around and under the
gauze on my bad eye. I thought I'd come and die right
there, but well-trained distance horse retired his galloping
tongue and gently laid me on my back on the high table
carpeted in black with gold zigzag designs (that's my job,
I notice those things).
Good eye closed fast, "Oh Mustapha, those lights hurt
your Frisco boy's good eye!"
Blotting out the sun with his white hooded head, lying
lightly on me, my black shoes poking his robed shins, soft
mouths (mine inside his), "Here my sweet Frisco Disco Boy,
I fix for you," his long foreleg swinging under the table,
a switch clicking. Out of large unseen speakers beat Gloria
Gaynor's ninety-minute fuck version of "I Will Survive,"
the anthem of baths (where's my disco whistle?) back in
the fun old days B.A. (Before AIDS). Now nobody fucks
anymore.
Browsing on my left ear and half of my fucking head,
low booming, "This is inspection table, I inspect and price
stupid killums, now I inspect you, very thorough, sexy
Crisco Frisco Boy! I wanna see it all, real real good, see

my big whip go up tight pink ass, come out your sucking white mouth, you like that, you want that, Beautiful California Whore – you want it all right now?!"

He certainly had his rap down, but then what else is there to do in Long Beach?

"I fuck your every hole many times, my California Blondie Hole – you feeling my big whip now, Surf Bitch?" as he slowly hump-moved up on me. More of a billyclub than a whip I'd say, as it rammed my panting junior police club whistle struggling frantically not to blow.

My aroused nose pushed down the express zipper on the front of his jellaba on top of me, then busied my face and mouth in his wiry black briar-patch chest I could not tongue to the end of, over acres of hard brambles protecting moaning blackberry pies on straining beefcake.

My hands fought his jellaba up over his buffalo head free-shooting long black coils, and snorting for my clothes. Slow, teasing, then heavy-handed hooves pulled off my job interview costume and tossed it on the floor, including black shoes and socks. For who can make real love in black business socks? (And distance of beeper from bed determines depth of committment?)

Naked hairy on each other, joyous whinnying, "Now! Now I see really see my California pink pussy boy!" moving me like air to my hands and knees, stallion mounting naturally from the rear, lifting my plump ass (so they tell me) for a too-big bird's eye touch to my constricting pink, most precious hole (or pink, blondie California pussy if you will).

Black gold carpeting on inspection table focused rapidly, time for clever quick defusing, "No, no, not yet Mustapha, you'll fuckin' kill me with that monster dong!" For who hasn't seen a horse hardong, if not felt one knock-knock-knocking against one's back door?

Stab at polite humor, "Why don't you just let me throw that thing over my shoulder, Mustapha honey, and burp

95

it for you?"

But experienced stud knew how to stretch my contracting cheeks with wet tongue kisses to entire plumpness, then Triple Crown Champion lifted my rosy winning circle to his kneeling lips, "Yes, yes, now! Now I kiss-kiss eat-eat pink pussy California! Ah, my Long Beach Department of Physical Education, ohhhh!" as hungry horse fell in – munching, chomping, snorting, spitting and sneezing, a stray California pussy hair up his broad nostril? While, "Oh my California pussy girl, oh mine all mine pink jewel with golden hair, oh so fine silk California pussy whore all mine!" plus deep tongue-thrusts killed my sphincter dead.

Bronco face-bucking my silked pink jewel box this way and that to aim his golden treasure more perfectly for his weep-feasting eyes. Then he ravished the whole spreading mother lode with his furiously rubbing face, his wet, slick, stubble-tickling chin, his thrilling hooked nose – shafra!

Overloaded pleasure circuits flew me to suns spotlighting our golden black gridiron, but horse's steady pull on my rearing rein settled me down to stand in front of him, his fat, blunt greased finger swallowed by my hungry rectum lips, yes!

After slow delicious fingering then fingerings, loud and teasy, "You want it all now, my Blondie Madonna Pussy?" (Leave her out of this!) "You just dying I stick my black monster in you? You ready take it all, my meter-stick, blondie pussy girl?" Chocolate cloves' final savage thrusts tickling my belly button from the inside.

My inaudible moaning, "Bring on the fucking Mack Truck!"

Instead, he reached around my waist and greased my modest Rolls Royce reeking of pouchouli; why why was he making me cum too much much too soon, pulling me falling over backwards onto his greased Monster Rubbered Everything, hairy claw whipping my high eminence flailing white offerings all over our black and gold altar-cloth hottening and stickening our pagan communion rock; we howled like savages.

Panting, pinned on top of him, I closed my eye to inspection lights as his throb held still, allowing me to become accustomed to the new heft inside me. His hands hairy-pressed my belly and thighs pushing him pregnant inside me. Suspended, breathing noted, I could feel it up in my throat and pushed down on him, wanting more; my bad eye felt fine.

Well-trained stud knew the parade lap was over, place your bets, starting gate opening without the bell unless you counted Gloria's disco thumps. Race fixed, of course, by horse become Leviathan jockey, slowly twisting his fat bullwhip in his tumbling burro scrambling back to the center of the track, to try new gaits and marathon riding positions, breaking all existing track records.

Burro let its milk down on thirsty jockey's licking face, Gloria screaming in the grandstand, "We won the fucking Perfecta! Ten times!"

But all attempts by horny burro to mount his rampy stallion's high proud haunches were rebuffed with angry snorts and even a few sharp nips. All the poor burro could do was tongue kiss-lick over vast brown bulges, then tease mass of curly black hair around the luscious brown pucker behind stallion's still rearing tail, stallion on belly with skittish hind legs barely apart hanging off the edge of his black and gold stable.

Calculating burro synchronized his skilled pointy hooves whacking horse's mighty bone with his practiced tongue braying dirty SoCal surfer shit while working furiously on tight horse's ass and his two dark hairy horse-apples swinging against burro's gasping Adam's apple.

"I really don't know how — how long we did it, or how long the other thing was, either."

Shifting on gray-black killumed bed, remembering to

97

hand Abdullah back his pipe, dish-tones, "Well, actually Mustapha did reveal to me his incredible but readily verifiable every-which-way measurements, but I'm no squeal queen, you're not gonna get every little detail outta me, my curious Abdullah — no matter how hard you fuck me."

Laughing his perfect but such little pony teeth, Abdullah dipped our tiny brass pipe into the round copper-brass-silver kif box to rekindle our interest. For my tawdry little story had not been told straight through; poor Abdullah's suffering had to be alleviated — gently, considering our respective medical conditions, but firmly, two times. All that blond California pussy shit got him hard and panting; also the heavy asswork part got us off, particularly all the tonguing, eating, chinning, nosing, etc. So I gave him a 911-modified asswork demonstration again — didn't this kif boy remember anything?

Then he reverently held the bark pipe for me as I drew on it, a nice touch. With rare real respect in his melodious español, "You really got a lot in your fuck adventure, locochón — ravished by a tender but menacing stranger with dirty and threatening but funny talk."

He chuckled admiringly; he was proud of me! "You know you made it like a giant dark satan fantasy, sliding into those hooved, shaggy beasts. Some good pagan imagery, and magical archetypes too."

Grabbing the pipe from him, "It was just a quickie, for Allah's sake! I wasn't composing your masters' thesis in fucking beast perversion, my most crackpot husband!"

The mock back in his soft laughter, "I think you have Ph.D. in sexual perversion specializing in unusual locales, locochón."

"Oh, wonderful! Let's just send my framed Fucking Diploma to my parents in Saliva so they can hang it on the parlor wall for when the lying Parson Weems comes to call!" But Abdullah probably didn't give a shit about Geo

98

Washington, much less his lying biographer, Parson Weems. Seriously back to the movie, "Your miscegenation was hot, big dark tongue, face, cock — toes?"

Firmly, "I don't allow feet in there, a girl has certain standards to uphold."

Surprised, "Oh. And your dark monster, huge of course, in tiny blond hole until it consumes him, and still can't get enough. A good comment on White Imperialism."

Falling back, bonking my head on the wall, "Oh give me a fucking break — Ouch! Now look what you made me do, my clumsiest wife!"

Patting me distractedly, "Third World refused to let First World fuck him in the ass, and good funny insults, too."

Disgusted cluck, "I thought I was gonna throw up. Mustapha would be a much better lay if he'd just shut up."

"But you should have kissed and licked, then sucked and swallowed his great, dark cock — like worshipping the primitive Third World you know — "

Snort, "I've still got my tonsils to protect, fuck your Third World!"

Earnest, leaning into me, "The verbal domination-submission was effective, but there should have been more physical S&M – light you know, like the Madonna video. Your eye bandage was a clever hint, but you should have shown how you got it."

"Your dumb friend Khalid wasn't invited."

"Maybe some leather masks or chains then, make it more threatening, surreal, and highlight the First-Third World reverse domination thing."

Pushing his pipe solely back into his own possession – into his nearly hairless skinny fingers on dull, scrawny hands; authoritatively, "I think Jung, Freud and Fellini are fucked. And that means you, Brother Abdullah, in case you didn't catch the imagery."

We talked about Us, of course, in abbreviated but startling relevations; a lot to catch up on for lovers recently met for the first time in this lifetime. Intimacies of our long skinny sausage pillow, its tube pillowcase with openings in both ends, like a defective white cotton condom for giants. Or a rearing Arabian stallion.

But Mustapha was not primary on my mind, although his massiveness was still warm-glowing around and deeply in my holiest of caverns — what a pleasant way to recall a lover and keep him with me for awhile. Though I was now with the most satisfying piece of my love puzzle, my doubts washed away in his presence that made me more "us" than I thought I could ever be.

Naked babes wedged together in his narrow bed, without even a sheet over our wounds, fucked-out bodies intertwining, but carefully, sore parts untouching.

Abdullah said he'd tried to kill himself when he was 19 because he was bored, life had no meaning, and he was curious how it would feel and what would come next. I assured him it all would probably happen soon enough, with someone else doing the job. He agreed.

Sleep drifting Abdullah in sweet español, "You know I really do love you, locochón. You're so off the wall – like Michael Jackson's album you know. Whew, there, I finally said it."

Snap awake español, "Yes, I fucking know Michael Jackson's album! What a way to say I love you, my tackiest wife. And Michael's a lot prettier than you, too, but then his bod's been cut on even more than yours!"

Regretful soft laughter, propping himself on his elbow which I groped at and bit, "What I mean, my sweetest life locochón, is that you're so open and accepting of everyone and everything which is rare in this world. You even fell for that stupid clown Mustapha posing as a real Arab in his jellaba, ha, with his head still stuck in Long Beach blondie pussy. Where is Long Beach, anyway?"

Elbow nips having no effect so trying gentle kisses, "In western–most Nebraska. But I think that was mostly just a physical thing between me and horsey-boy. It will be nice to speak real Americano at work — today, those were the first conversations in fast natural English I've had since I've been here. Well, with Ms. Dawson mostly; I guess Mustapha and I didn't really get to talk."

Grabbing, turning me over, hobby horse reared and mounted me; fast grease, condom, in easily, I guess I was pretty loose by now.

Full in, stopped: "Now we're in a better position to talk, my almost virgin wife."

Slow pumping, long slender gentle love for all ages; serious, "I really love you. I really do. There, I said it in simple sentence without dependent clause."

Moaning, shifting to face to face — only slowing, not breaking our rhythm — we were the same height and were long enough so that faces together was our natural position. Sensitive nimble fingers greased my rising again, such a busy day today, I'll read and rest up all day mañana but that's what I say every day.

Between pantings, "Th-ank you my Ab-dul-lah! for your sim-simple dec-lar-a-shun of love–uh! Stop putóning me un ratito, señor."

He stopped in the extreme in position. "You know I love you the best here, my close-to-perfect Abdullah." Low, "Except you're probably gonna get fuckin' murdered!" I tried to painfully pinch his thruster with a last-gasp squeeze of my sphincter that had, alas, gaily surrendered to Long Beach State several hours ago.

Slow moving in me again, heroic endurance a Moroccan survival trait, matter-of-fact in his slow español, "I never say 'I love you' to anyone because it's such camelshit mierda — nowadays people say it even before they fuck. And it brings me bad luck, I say I love you today, tomorrow you go away," whamming me too hard. I resisted, he

101

slowed, his dominance established again.

Beautiful Abdullah's full-sail brown nose rubbed mine on the dark bed, our wet faces pressed, impressed that the first time we wept together this lifetime we so naturally remembered our pain.

My heart in him chilled, "I'm going to be the grieving widow again. Fuck! Why do you always get to die?"

Moving in me again in beat to his bat-pitched "Dee-dee dee-dee, Dee-dee-dee" (he'd watched too much TV de España as a kid).

His light mock back, "Oh, you mean my little shafra scratches."

"Not exactly scratches, asshole!"

Sometimes I was too loud for face to face, so he smoothly rolled me onto my skidmarked belly again without missing a beat, lying lightly on my back to protect his sweat-drenched bandaged belly.

Completely out, slow back in in in oh! as he laughed at his silly fuckchild, "Be real asshole. If they'd really wanted to kill me, you would have found my guts hanging out all over the floor over there."

Stopping his ass with my slapping hands behind me like preparing for a dive, "You mean you weren't going to die anyway when I so resourcefully piled those books and clothes on your belly? I mean you were really bl-bleeding, something awful, Abdullah!"

Gentle giant hands soothed my shaking, he didn't even try to move in me anymore, just in there rock–solid connected forever.

"But – but," blubbering, "but I didn't really save your life after all!"

Shy Abdullah whispered, so no one outside in the sleeping Medina could hear, "Except for right now, and every day the rest of our lives, my one perfect wife-husband, you."

¡Simón! I moved him in me again, until too rápidamente perfectamente, más explosiones pues. O diosas, when will I have enough for one day? (I'd better be careful or I'd turn into a pathetic nymphomaniac riddled with AIDS and lots of pissed-off ex-lovers.)

We were joy sweaty again, brave Abdullah moaning his painful belly, my bad eye throbbing, as we groped for our respective packs of pain pills in the dark, chugged down with agua Sidi Ali. Then un poco más TV by candlelight, mock laughing me, "It only seemed like a lot of blood to you, Americano pink pussy boy. But you didn't see it pumping out of me, did you?"

Pink pussy boy abashed, "Oh — no artery hit, and your nursey-friend Sueád was on her way up here for a little, uh, social visit to my most whorey husband; I'm glad I didn't save your life!"

Slight whack up the side of my head with his, propped on flickering pillows, "But why did he only 'scratch' you, as you so macholy put it?"

His sighing arm around me, evenly, "It was supposed to be a warning, a little family business problem. I'm the favorite of my father and easy to get at — puto loco in the city — my family lives down the coast in their well protected, ah, house."

"Their fucking Barbary Pirate Kasabah!" (fort in Arabic)

Laugh, gentle roughing, "They're not that rich, they're just businessmen, a little of this and a little of that."

"Diversified Smuggling, Inc!"

Sad laugh, "Anyway, the guy hired to tickle me with his shafra, well, he was pretty drunk — "

"I thought Arab assassins were supposed to watch TV before doing their dirty deeds."

"See how you imperialists have corrupted us and rendered us ineffective?"

My quick strike to Third World's most vulnerable point threatened to render howling Abdullah ineffective for at least 10 or 15 minutes.

Bowing dark kinks, "OK, I surrender, my Ayatollah Bush. I admit my camel assassin was, ah, caught down in the Grand Souk in a cafe, watching heavy television in the noblest Arab tradition."

"Oh! That's how your nursey friend hurt her arm. I never did believe the motorcycle wreck story — too coincidental even for Tanger. I figured Sueád for a karate instructor all along."

Mock wonder, "Oh you must shut up, my too smart wife."

"Oh, okay. That sounds like a swell deal."

Laugh-rocking me gingerly against his taped belly, "You're my perfect everything, my locochón baby. You come to Paris with me now."

Rock stopped, "I can't go on a vacation now, my foolish, wonderful Abdullah. Tomorrow's my first day of work — hmmm, I wonder if Ms. Dawson will have what's-his-name instruct me in killum inspecting, a little nightball under the lights?"

Solemnly holding me tight, "That's just what I mean. That's why you go to Paris with me now, not vacation — to live. I'm going to Paris to study and you live with me. Just you and me and our beautiful Paris, I show you the everything!"

Quick sit-up straight, no parts touching except my angry hands squeezing Abdullah's severely-hickied slim brown neck. "Are you fucking loco-nuts? I mean after heaven, our little yin-yang gangbang of the past few days — days? Already we gotta continue our Battle of the Eons? I'm-not-going-to-no-fucking-big-expensive-Paris-where-I-don't-even-fucking-speak-the-language! Not when I'm home in heaven here in perfect Tanger!"

Patiently peeling my fingers from around his neck and wrapping them around his strong point, "My father and I decided I should go. He always wanted me to study there; I did the best of my family in school and there are plenty of them here to run their dumb business – too many if you count all the uncles and cousins." Shrugging, "I'm finished here playing stupid streetboy games, but it was fun and I learned a lot."

"No more watching 'your friend's' Marlboro stand?" He moved my hand on him again. Don't these horny Tangerinos ever quit?

"Can I have the little incense burner-change pot to remember you by?"

Serious kissing, he hadn't given up yet, "We'll put it on our fireplace mantle in our beautiful Paris apartment to remember our first meeting and honeymoon forever. My father gives me money to study, but not for this kind of life. You be my only wife there and you won't even have to get a job; I be strong camel husband and support your everything."

Now that was tempting. But not working is usually more work than working, and being supported means being squashed. So tonelessly, "When do you leave, Abdullah?"

Abdullah blew out the candle and sighed all over me, "I stay here maybe one month or so until my stomach heals. And until I persuade you, the only love of my sad camel life, to accompany me. You're like real father to me."

"Fuck you, Jack! You be the father!" and we clung crying together like found children lost in the dark.

HUNTING IN THE MEDINA

The next few weeks flew blurred. I mostly worried about Joe Montana's elbow surgery – could jaunty Mormon Steve Young lead my 49'ers to the land of milk and honey again?

I was saving the daily 85 dirham for my nice hotel room by shacking up with my perfectly adequate lovelust. And I didn't charge recovering Abdullah a single dirham for my services as nurse and internal body guard.

He still nagged me about Pairs but without much gusto; of course he understood why puto Chicano must remain Tangerino, at least until the luster rubbed off, but so far my adopted city was luster-rubbing me gloriously, when it wasn't hurting me. Or overheating me, but then it was still hot September, 80° - 90° in the daytime but cool at night. They say the rest of the year, except summers, is delightful, like a warmer San Pancho – a ver.

And Paris only three hours by plane, so we were eagerly planning our first bodymindsoul bang in Gay Left-Bank Paree over the Channukah-Christmas holidays; international Tanger celebrated everything. How about Halloween and Chinese New Years – the biggest holidays in San Francisco, Gaysian Capital of the World.

But I was passing too many handkerchiefing hours twitching in low, hot cafes, drinking too many of my and Khalid's cervezas Speciales du Maroc, watching prodigious Khalid TV, waiting, waiting to be shown apartments allegedly for rent by cousins of friends of wheeling-dealing Khalid, the King of the Cafe.

"Oh yes, your apartment," interrupting his impassioned Arabic conversation with idle cafe hangers. "Sí, sí, you must be patient, my sweatiest wife, for today La Palabra Es La Paciencia – Y Por El Hombre Real, La Palabra Es –"

"Chingoza mierdaza chingote chingón burrito-burrón

ignorantísimo!!" forgetting my still slightly discolored eye as I recited the popular Mexicano idiom, which required extensive explaining, complete with graphic gestures. In simple español Tangerino with pronouns even, for precise conjugation of Spanish verbs was not a local custom, at least in feckless cafes. And we sang in crippled English:

"California here we come
Right back where we started from
Where bowers of flowers bloom in the sun
Each morning at dawning, birdies sing and everything
A sunkissed miss says don't be late
That's why I can hardly wait
Open up your Golden Gate
To Missión Acción we come!"

Their pet Americano monkey was entertaining the lazy cafe crowd again and we were all laughing again and that was the problem again.

I put my foot down on Khalid's literal neck one night at the baths after several days of fruitless cafe bullshit. (Perfect boss Ms. Dawson had given me time off to apartment hunt, Liz-chuckling, "It'll be a trip for you," when I declined her offer of Mustapha's help. I didn't want that sleezeball SoCal airqueen in jellaba drag garbaging my ear anymore. He had been a perfect one night stand.)

"Oh, thanks, Ms. Dawson, but I've already retained the services of a free-lance apartment rental consultant. He assures me we can wrap it all up in one day."

Raucous laughter tossed masses of black and silver curls, "You mean one of your sleazy street boys? I told you it would be a trip!"

(Why are they always right?)

Khalid and I went regularly to our favorite cheap homeboy hamman, a clean warm fucksite. We did everything there, but coolly, under bathing partner's slipping wet underwear in our nearly dark washing cubicle, open, but way down on the end around the corner.

My large pink foot on his struggling then passive well-washed, shiny brown neck in our dim, tiled cubicle, "When, pues, do we quit TV fucking around in cafes everyday and find my perfect apartment, cabrón?" After today's predictable fiasco when my Apartment Consultant had assured me, "Oh, she my good friend, more like a sister to me, very trustworthy, has your perfect apartment, my naggiest wife."

Trustworthy sister-friend showed up at our TV beach cafe extremely drunk two hours late, and oh yes, some friends of hers were crashing indefinitely in my perfect apartment.

My foot pressing harder on his laughing neck, didn't he understand torture? "I'm fucking sick and tired of saying 'Incháallah' (if Allah wills) a thousand times a day about this apartment nothing, Chingoni" (Italianizing mi Mexicano). "Tomorrow we no see apartment, no dirham for baby Khalid; you are working on commission now."

For I had been paying my Expert Apartment Locator, as he'd titled himself, 50-100 dirham a day for his time and efforts – plus paying this, paying that on our long tedious cafe runs. Lazy me let him do everything, for I knew the perfect apartment would eventually pop up, it always did. Plus I got my money's worth out of Khalid in many ways – for a best friend savvy on the street level is crucial in any new place. Poor Abdullah was wounded, plus he lived too much in his mind and books to help me much with reality, except my morale.

Proud Khalid had gloated the first time I called him Mi Profesor de Cafe y Calle (street). He shouted it out, hailing me in Arabic to the amused crowd in another beach cafe we were mired in at the time. I wished he wouldn't do that, I was the center too much; fierce tender love took me out.

Khalid's neck escaped my angry foot and he started doing rude things with a bar of warm soap under my wet underwear, but coolly. Playhurt, "You know you never appreciate the everything I do for you until I'm dead Por Dios, then no more strong husband Khalid to protect you, then you see what thieves those other boys are. I keep warning you but you talk to the every puto on the street that talk to you Por Dios!"

For there was intense competition among the informal guides (without Tourist Agency photo ID cards) for their "foreigner," whom they would sometimes fiercely drag away with sharp, mean Arabic aimed at encroaching puto TV men threatening to grab their grubstake.

"You know not poor Khalid's fault again today, why throw the blame at me?" his slick finger moaned in as his other hand expertly jacked me out of my Hanes. "La chica muy loco pues, muy borracho (drunk), el culpa (blame) no se mío pues."

Polite low public baths' panting, "Then it must be Allah's will, he's slower than fucking Dios. Oh, slower! Yes, like that. But busy Allah and Dios don't work on commission, like my sextoy Khalid does, starting tomorrow."

Disgusted fast whipping creamed my little lust dream prematurely; the next day we saw two apartments.

It had suddenly occurred to my resourceful young consultant to walk captive Americano to an apartment rental agency one block from Boulevard Pasteur. Oh, they had them here, too! Blink, I think slower in TV-landia.

After my passport data were duly noted, the rental agent from the small office and Arabic-speaking Khalid began to drag me towards modern "safe" buildings around Le Boulevard, near my ex-hotel.

"Stop! Fuckin' Aye, man! The architecture here is European, Mediterranean? Nice Moorish touches like lines and keyhole arches but I-want-to-live-in-Arabia! In the Medina, I told you a thousand times already, Khalid putonazo!"

The skinny, intense rental agency man cringed and ducked our head-bangs and harsh words, but my strong Kansaño hands kept him walking between us down the crowded sidewalk because I wanted to speak directly to him. The rental agent spoke perfect Spantalian because he'd studied at an Italian school here, and no way would I allow my high Mexicano to be diluted or distorted by Khalid's tenseless TV Spanish through his rosy dirham glasses.

My patting arm around the agent, reassuring friendly biz, "Ah señor, mi señorito muy buenito mío, you're going to help me I know, simón, I mean sí," (they don't know simón here). "You save my very life today, muy amigazo, mi pobre mamá thanks you that her poor son won't have to sleep on the street tonight." He bowed his head, but I omit La Sacrada Virgin here.

"My perfect apartment must be a small place, not a big place, with one small kitchen and one small bathroom with hot water shower, and one small to medium just-one-room for both living and sleeping. Plus a humble balcony or rooftop terrace would be much appreciated. And, mi señorito tan bueno, I won't pay one chingado centavo more than 600 dirham a month," an egregious bargaining lie we both realized, but it was like the first blow in a fight or the first kiss on a date.

"But listen very carefully, mi señor muy mi-íto, I must live in the Medina, yes the Medina, THE FUCKING MEDINA YES!"

Biz-calmed agent patted my back down Le Boulevard, "Ah but mi Señor Americano muy bueno, fino − La Medina, she is very trashy and wet, like the pig!"

"Just what I want!" heavy-handed Americano whack startled the agent's back as I led them down to the Medina,

110

Khalid elbowing pedestrians trying to keep his head between ours.

"You see, my most understanding señor, I'm just a simple farmboy from Kansas, that's a state even bigger than Texas." The agent sighed at giant America, like a heavy she-camel pregnant with twins.

"And after all the Indian villages in Latin America, why, I feel right at home in the slums of the world, from Tepito to Klong Thuey."

The agent stopped me abruptly, his gray eyes wide in his light wrinkled face, "Oh no, mi Señor Americano so sorrowfully misguided, La Medina she is no slum, no no, very ancient, many historical monument with beautiful white Kasabah at top!" gesturing wildly. "Now you understand? All right, I show you perfect apartment there; La Medina she have too many fine apartments for our Amigos Americanos," patting me down the street packed with cars and people towards the Grand Souk market and plaza − which reminded me only fleetingly of the night of Abdullah's scarlet tickle and the dirty little Marlboro boy.

Poor kid, he was probably a sniffer. Here as everywhere in poor countries, orphaned and no-school kids used small profits from selling cigarettes or whatever on the streets to buy glue, paint thinner, gasoline and who-knows-what for the small rags you saw them putting to their noses. One kid hissed and lightly spat on me once when I refused him a cigarette; he looked about ten years old. I was smoking at the time, of course, trustworthy adult teaching hypocrisy. Plus he probably only wanted to sell it to buy glue ration? I felt guilty for not giving him the cigarette, but the spit was neat.

We jumped out into the slow car-crowded street to walk down the hill to the Grand Souk − single-file, Khalid grabbing my arm too hard, "Wait!" as I dragged him along. "Por Dios I know that man all my life, he's my best friend except for you of course, he knows your perfect Medina apartment Por Dios, see how I help you, your best friend Khalid?!"

Sweaty redface wresting arm free from him, muttering "Tabone deemak!" (Fuck off; literally fuck your mother in Arabic, the gravest insult; societies that oppress women worship mothers and virgins.)

I strode and handkerchiefed faster not to lose my wiry agent darting crowds on the street, zeroing in on my perfect apartment in the Medina.

It was a nightmare, of course. Missing landlords, missing keys, squirming in tiny Medina tourist shops, expertly marveling over inexpensive treasures I'd seen a million times before here, but trying to impress proprieters who were landlords or knew landlords or something about my perfect apartment just waiting for me there. If we could only wait a little longer, come back tomorrow or in three or four days. A friend of a cousin was sure to have something.

Twisting through the quiet Medina streets, no cars, only occasional slow motorcyles piled high with huge paper bags thrusting brown loaves of French bread. Or a three wheeled motorcycle cart carrying stacks of cut leather for luscious soft tourist anythings, hand-manufactured in six-man Medina leather shops with the doors open.

I tried, mostly unsuccessfully, to remember landmarks, store signs like the Lion Boutique, which became Lion Street, for I couldn't remember the Moroccan street names written in both French and Arabic on small metal signs flat on the sides of houses and buildings. The modern street lights were attached to the old stucco buildings, too, as were the electric wires – no room for poles. And when the electrical wires ran overhead in the middle of the street, they almost touched roofs overlapping the street on both sides, at least casting shadows on the hot stone footpaths.

The Medina streets followed the ancient trails winding around the highest hill up from Tanger Bay, protected by the fortress Kasabah overlooking the Mediterranean sparkling blue to the mountains of Spain, only 14 foggy kilometers away.

I was into Barbary Pirates now, fuck Roman soldiers. Ah, Abdullah's noble family giving him, thus me, money now. Whoops, not paying attention again, I bumped into my two eager leaders who were pounding on and yelling through yet another heavy wooden door.

At last, an actual key from a smiling pink-jellaba'ed woman whom I greeted friendly but formally, "L'bas," reverently slapping my chest with entire right hand – serious biz.

She led us several sweaty blocks to my Promised Land: a six-story walkup (most Medina buildings are only two to four stories). It had too many rooms for a bachelor (pushy Khalid thought it was muy perfecto), was fully equipped and furnished too cushy nice, and in the stratosphere at 4,000 dirham a month.

My carefully enunciated, "Sokran, Salaamalíacomb, Señora," (Thank you, may peace be with you), then touching my forehead, lips, and chest with fingertips together, a beautiful Arabic thank you gesture. Then I tumbled down six flights of narrow marble steps, sweat-ready to fight.

The last price I heard her shouting on the way down was 1500, "¡Sólo milquientos Señor!" Walking-away an effective bargaining tool – upper body leaning and jerking steadily away, while dem feets is jus' stutterin' down dere. But fleeing madly really crashes the price, just ask Wall Street.

Two black and two gray wide eyes speed-reading me on the quiet street, my sopping handkerchief only spreading the sweat around on my face, neck and rounded pink, hairy belly I displayed – pulling up my nice shirt with buttons even that I'd worn for a good impression in quiet, cool apartment interviews, all wet now.

113

Quiet dramatic beginning, "Mis muy buenos señores y guías (guides). I thought I had very carefully made myself perfectly clear like Tricky Dicky," (they didn't get it, it was for me), "that my perfect 1000 dirham apartment must have, must have one small kitchen one, one small bathroom one with hot hot shower one, and one, only one-one-one other room, to live and to sleep one very alone one!" Still mopping, "Fuck the balcony and terrace."

"Oh, but of course!" Khalid and the wily white Tangerino agent were one in their huddle of startling Arabic revelations. Yes! Speeding single-file, corkscrewing through the Medina once more, yes, they finally understood. I didn't believe it for a second.

To another tourist shop and then to another house for key woman, with a sit-down in a third floor family living room, very comfortably if a little brightly furnished. Large television set and VCR off, flowery español pleasantries with cozy diminutives for brightly jellaba'ed ladies: "Oh yes I just love Tanger, people so nice, cool nights, you can walk everywhere it's so chiquitito − toditito es muy cerquitito − " to blissy, appreciative laughter.

Then silver tray and dry glasses were brought in with agua Sidi Ali and the big-size Coca Cola bottle. "Oh señora, the Coca Cola is excellent, you are a wonderful cook!" eliciting predictable but exhilarating laughter, for she was taking us several more sweaty blocks to − my most imperfect apartment.

A small shabby, windowless room, no kitchen, not even a sink in the corner to piss in, bath down a dirty dark hall. My ex-hotel 1,000 times better than this! But the situation gave me a real-life opportunity to practice some of my latest Arabic phrases on my deflated apartment consultants:

"You donkey goat-piss, camel-fucking shit on your mothers pigsuckers!" or something like that, as I once again explicitly detailed my exact apartment specifications, in Mexicano muy chingote.

Scrambling down hot steps again; the kind Coca Cola woman in shiny gray jellaba, who had innocently shown us her cheap rooming house, seemed shocked at how quickly I'd picked up Arabic and how thoroughly I could express my emotions in español. Maybe I should get a job at the fucking U.N.

Desperate Khalid clung to my flailing wet arm as I started up some stone steps towards Abdullah's. I kinda knew where I was, the hills helped here, plus I could ask any kid the way to the Marlboro Man's room who got shafra'ed, for Abdullah was enjoying his ten minutes of notoriety in the Medina. But only because of who his family was, he insisted, when I'd threatened to sic Geraldo Rivera on him during one of our meaningless squabbles.

Soft groaning turned me around and brought me back down the step street to the wizened rental agent, moaning over working more than half a day without earning a single dirham for his arduous efforts and good will for Señor Bueno Americano tan olvidoso (so forgetful). Because his poor children needed their leche, of course; probably not half as bad as their poor old dad needed some strong TV.

So, smiling, I dropped a ten dirham bill into his shocked hand. Insult and humiliation can be powerful bargaining weapons if the opponent is already down, you intend never to do business with him again, and there is no physical peril (dumb Khalid would protect me).

The nimble agent and I wrestled the ten dirham bill between us, he trying to shove it back into my hand – with mutual grunts and whinings about 100 dirham for leche and zero dirham for fucking up. By the time I plunked a fifty on him, he was relieved and grateful, running off promising perfection on the morrow. No más morrows!

Oh, to be back in San Pancho where everything's so easy; all you need to find a perfect, cheap apartment there is to speak Chinese or Spanish. Or even back in Saliva, where you could rent a mansion for $50 a month; the only

115

problem was you had to live there.

Only problem here was the large, ingratiating puppy standing before me, slapping hands with his most talented student for becoming a real Tangerino at last – for humiliating poor old rental agent. Though poor old agent had sped through the Medina the fastest and sweated nary a drop. I wondered what channel he watched?

At the bottom of the stone steps, I touched my slightly discolored right eye; it had been through the palette, I didn't want him here anymore.

Grabbing my arm too hard, imploring, "Wait! Por Dios blah blah blah," habits becoming increasingly irritating to meal ticket slipping away.

Ear-coo, "We go together now to Abdullah's room, cool off Por Dios, take shower in sink, smoke a little kif. Then we put you in the middle, you be Lucky Pierre, calm your nerve. We work too hard today, my angriest wife."

No words, I backed away from his selfish grabbings, and tripped over the first stone step, bonking the back of my head on the rest.

Hordes of Roman soldiers in gray Canadian goose wings, flying south in a dark V to their perfect Mexicano apartments, honked sweet love songs over unconscious, Unlucky Pierre.

But Lucky Pierre awoke, lying on Abdullah's gray and black killumed bed, sandwiched between his two Tangerinos, their mighty shafras luckily still sheathed. Abdullah was touching an ice-towel to my head, Khalid groan-kissing the rest of me; where were my clothes?

My head sharp throbbing, low wails – as much from frustration and humiliation as pain – brought Abdullah's long hand softly over my mouth with his sweet tongue lightly massaging the goose egg growing on the back of my head.

I was cool, Abdullah's hand off my mouth, tender head

massage mumbles, "Oh, my sweetest honeyfig wife, I must beg your forgiveness for what my psychotic camel driver, my ex-best friend has done to you, again!"

Nervous Khalid, wordless for once, directed his kissing groans to my most vulnerable point. No! I can't, not now, dying and everything, and after I had hated him so – I only thought, as the absence of any nervous system connection between my brain and cock became readily apparent again.

Abdullah diverted my attention back up to his sweet, perfumey kif mouth in mine, "Good news medicine for you, locochón. Sueád has found your perfect apartment for you. A sublet from a friend studying in Barcelona. It's furnished, up from here near the Kasabah, two small rooms with a terrazza overlooking the Mediteranean for you, and a small kitchen, I don't know the price."

Startled Khalid quickly moved to tingly rimming and Abdullah went down on me, the best medicine. I shoulda stood in bed today.

Perfect Apartment Pierre jumped up to take a carefully aimed celebratory hardong piss in the clean chamber pot like a strong Roman soldier, leaving my toasted slices looking anxiously at their escaped BLT moaning, touching the back of his head and pissing straight into the wall. Abdullah considered again letting his pesky soulmate piss in his sink in the corner, but it was such a filthy barbarian custom; at least you didn't wash your face on the wall.

Staggering back to the bed, I carefully fixed my own kif medication in the bark pipe and played with my own bone, for my missing Lucky Pierre pieces were busy bouncing around the small room, getting their daily physical and emotional exercise, one hook nose slapping the other, shouting Arabic insults about shit and their mothers, I think (I take notes in cafes but they were screaming too fast).

Poor Khalid on defense, losing possession to Perfect

Abdullah deep in his own territory, and fearing a crippling roughing his mealticket penalty.

But then, I'm not one to talk much about my lovers, or compare them, yuk, that's so tacky — I mused, deep into my own barkwood glow fantasies, perfect Roman goose egg hatching my own Tangerino home at last.

Tabone Deemak (fuck off) world! (After I get to be Lucky Pierre just one more time.)

By the crack of dawn, 11 a.m., Los Tres Amigos Pierres were sink-cleaned, cafe au laited and French breaded (Abdullah's father buy, Khalid fly), and piling laughing out of Abdullah's room — up stone step footpaths to Sueád's perfect sublet for me.

My goose egg had been medicated with Abdullah-Khalid cream and another of Sueád's free supply of pain killers. Abdullah's scab-lined belly was down to band-aids now, he hadn't even gotten stitches, how could I have been so silly to think I'd saved his life? But oh, there had been so much scarlet greasing his noble black belly hair — don't think about it, breathe-concentrate on Sueád's pain killer kicking in and all your own fucking wounds.

This part of the Medina was too high and steep for most tourists; their shops and restaurants were down on the easy-walking flats, like my Lion Street. Up here, Tangerinos lived in Oh Little Town of Bethlehem, which I sang Saliva Baptist-sweet to my amused but impressed amigos.

Khalid naturally came along, for apartment hunts here were conducted in packs — with friend, friend's friend, agent maybe two, owner maybe more. The story was that Moroccans preferred to rent to foreigners in the belief that they'd keep the place up better and pay higher rent, the latter surely true. Tanger was like San Pancho — too many people wanted to live there plus goddamn rich tourists drove up the prices. (I was Tangerino man pues!)

118

Single-file past a few idle teenagers in loose white pinstriped candoras (jellabas without the hood), leaning against pastel mud walls with colored wood doors, smiling hellos. Fewer aggressive "guides" up here off the beaten tourist path.

Plus I was so obviously taken, and our infectious joy had to convince grinning witnesses that we were lovers, not just the typical tourist with hustling guides. Though Khalid was hustling me and I was hustling Abdullah's father and Ms. Dawson (I felt guilty receiving salary while apt-hunting, so I tried to go in for at least two or three hours every two or three days).

My thoughtful attempts to help grunting Abdullah (poor boy needed more rest) up the steepest section of steps were laughingly shoved away; we were pain separating again, dee-dee-dee-dee.

Abdullah and Khalid Arabic arguing as we climbed, ah, their morning warm-up. I made them switch to Spanish, which always disintegrated into Spanabic, but still I could understand too much: they were arguing about their Señor Pierre Americano again — more ridiculous and boring than flattering.

Piteous self-righteousness, "I met him first Por Dios so long time ago, his first best friend, nurture him since first night he arrive Tanger. Poor man I take his hurting legs to hamman, teach him make beautiful love there, cure him his best friend Khalid!"

Mock Abdullah, "You steal all his dollars Americanos, then push crippled old man over wall to your camelshit-house — la coche abandonada en los palos muertos (dead sticks), especialamente el palito muertito tuyito!" (your little little little dead stick!)

Eager suffering con't: "Por Dios I help him buy simple necessities, save his money, every day all day help him find apartment, be very patient not hit him when he disgrace me in public with terrible Mexicano words, and now in

119

Arabic too Por Dios!"

Stoic Khalid ignored our whoops and derisive punches (fun to smack him around a little as long as Abdullah was there to protect me). "Poor man's job pay him little money for rich Americano, now you rich daddy's boy not think about money make him buy expensive airplane ticket and fly all the way to Paris too expensive spend all his traveler check just to visit his puto Marhueco, when Tanger have every puto Marhueco right here just for him!"

Sometimes Khalid made good sense. And I hated how Abdullah yelled back at him, so smug superior, "I'm paying for his fucking plane ticket and he'll stay in my luxury apartment on the camelfucking West Bank so go shit up your mother's cunt, cigarette boy!"

Khalid grabbed me protectively, angry tongue cluck; sympathetically, "Even worse! Now everyone know he's Abdullah's paid puto, disgrace good Americano name and poor old mother suffering in La Saliva de Kansas! He walk down Le Boulevard everyone laugh at Abdullah's puto, lose his job, have to live in la coche abandonado, no no! Honest Khalid save his only wife!" squeezing me for dirham.

Fire black eyes and blazing arms shoving behind my head, so I scooted away to protect my tender goose egg, now down to a hard boiled duck egg, and I wanted to keep it that way. Guess I'd have to expand my lie, to head banging around inside douche-urinal? That should play to the Yellow River crowd.

Abdullah's almost-in-español screaming, "We're each other's fuckass putos and we don't give a flying fuck who knows it, you fuedalistic son of a shitshecamel! It's my father's money, so you're saying he's my father's puto – you're a disgrace to your whole turdcamel family!"

Now that was an idea! If I were Abdullah's father's puto, I'd get the Barbary Pirate job for sure! And if he was half the manwoman his son was –

Enough Spanabic racket, so I politely requested ("Shut the fuck up!") they change the channel all the way back to the Arabic station so I wouldn't have to listen. Fantasy time: subject, perfect sublet, probably another cruel Tangerino hoax, "Twice-digested camel dung," I made puzzled Khalid teach me in a beach cafe.

Sueád seemed a trustworthy karate instructor posing as efficient camelnurse and apartment locator.

Abdullah had gotten me into camel imagery – he explained it was an intellectual Arab extreme of his Cultural Conflict; an opposite extreme being, while passionately rimming me, mock(?) moaning, "Madonna! Oh Ma*donna!*"

I patiently explained to him that he was not Culturally Conflicted, but rather Culturally Complimentary – like Filipinos, who are easy citizens of the world due to their varied racial and cultural influences. Told him an old Flip joke: "Spanish and American colonialism for Filipinos was like living 500 years in the convent and 50 years in Hollywood!"

Of course Abdullah already knew this, except the Filipino joke which he loved as a satiric jibe at repressive religion and materialistic whore imperialism. I agreed.

But he preferred the term Culturally Conflicted because it sounded more tragic, and an Arab boy in Paris needed his every edge, he said.

Mis dos amigos now calmados, exercise finished, joshing as we climbed. The few seconds of relative peace allowed me to remember incidents for my secret travel journal, with the good parts in confusing (to me) code, so the Moroccan secret police, when they slipped into my hotel room (they probably weren't allowed in Abdullah's) to rifle its contents and steal my TV, wouldn't find out what King Hassan already knew, watching me in all those seedy TV cafes and my hamman de fuck. Although the policemen (no women) here did seem mellower and happier than your average Tangerino. Their tips were probably better.

And what exactly was my old trick Mustapha's job at Dawson y Dawson? Why did he seem like a cop when he was probably only Kinky Liz's rent-a-stallion? His infrequent visits there consisted of brief mutterings with Ms. Dawson up in the office or quick visits to the basement, where I'd grope his hardness, even when it was soft, under his rich, shiny, jellaba drag.

He'd laugh sarcastically, slapping my hot hand away and dirty-talking me, "Oh no, my great black whip not enough to satisfy Frisco nymphoboy. No no, you want my this up your saggy pink ass," grinding his wrecker's-ball brown hairy fist against my quickly contracting, definitely not saggy cheeks under my black Levi's. Another advantage of this job, no dress-code — a ridiculous word if you think about it.

Mustapha's dull power-tripping made me swear if I ever fucked him again it would be with a slipped hit of acid in him and a gag. Our infrequent grope-squabbles amused my shipping and receiving co-workers in the basement, a handful of silly boys to toothless old men, on-call for a few days low paid work at a time; they understood español when they wanted to.

In my moments at Dawson y Dawson Exports, I was proud hewer and drawer of killums, Berber weavings done by women at home. I exclaimed in Mexicano over zap-colored tight warps and weaves, so similar to Latin American Indian weaving with fascinating design differences, under the bright inspection lights. I sometimes recalled the hot sex on my black and gold killum-carpeted workbench, which meant more to me now than that horse's ass Mustapha ever did.

Liz was a perfect boss, friendly, encouraging, leaving me completely alone to play in my basement where I helped pack killums for export and unbundle warm heavy-smelling new ones to inspect — from fascinating, real Moroccan cities (Tanger so international) that I couldn't wait to visit. Like Fes.

SWEET PONY BOY ALI

Especially Fes, where my latest perfect lovelust Ali was surely dreaming of me, as I dreamed about him, only six hot hours south by train (he traveled at night, fourth class, 42 dirham). Stolen hour quickies with sweetest country boy was perfect therapy for my recently hectic City life. And Ali asked me for nothing, nada, nunca never.

Actually, Fes was a large city, but slower and gentler than hustling, grasping Tanger, insisted poor Ali who had recently had his wallet lifted in the market here. So I became his body guard Tangerino.

We nastied our new love slickly but quietly in dim washing cubicle down at the end around the corner at favorite fuck hamman, fresh squeezed OJ before and after, thanking highest lowlife Profesor Khalid de Calle y Cafe, in absentia again.

Short dark, stocky Ali, Strong Pony of Arabia! (I wasn't big enough for a horse yet.) He was so sensitive and considerate, too − within minutes into our first meeting of grins melting, I two quick but dignified, for we were on Le Boulevard, pelvic thrusts: "You want to?"

Wide toothy smile, hand smoothing his groined Levi's, "Oh no problem that!"

The only problem was we couldn't talk: four languages between us but not one in common: me Eng and Span, he Arabic and French, for only Northcoast Moroccans pick up español. So we chose to miscommunicate in inglés, for serious Ali would be starting his second year at Fes U as an English major.

He seemed not to have had much oral practice in his English classes, however, as in cheap restaurant conversation (guess who paid, with torturously slow English over-enunciation falling into soft black save-me pony eyes?):

Me,   "Much food here."
Him,   "Yes much food."
Etc., "Food good in Tanger, very good food here."
       "Yes food very good Tanger."
       "Now, in Soviet Union – many problem with food."
       "Yes, Soviet Union, what?"

But our oral communication was vastly improved by my sadly neglected French-English pocket dictionary. After considerable practice, we could communicate a complex but comprehensible sentence in well under five minutes. Sometimes.

"No Ali no! Me no say you like woman, no! Me say you have most manliest, most thickest, bushy-haired asshole I ever sank my fuckin' face or life into!" demonstrating frantically under his slick red bikini at the hamman – action the truest teacher any old fuck afternoon.

Plus poor dictionary pages getting wet, gummy and stuck together by bright KY-cum fingers. Grooving new lovelust, any words thrilling, amusing and fine. Enchantment licking dark pony features jutting into me, laughing oversized shining gappy protruding perfect pony teeth – fuckin' teeth get me every time.

But Ali saved from being a younger version of Mustapha by one-hundred pounds and his humorous sensitivity; he'd never stomp his polite pony hoof in my pink satin jewel box.

Like so many young people around the world, Ali dreamed of going to "America," as they called it with a reverent ring. As a Chicano by osmosis (injection?), I resented that, telling them there were three Americas, South, Central and North; and they, like good Canadians, should call it "The States." El Otro Lado (The Other Side) was the appropriate Mexicano, but that would be geographically confusing here – El Otro Lado, Algeria? Mauritania?

125

Of course these youth can't get U.S. tourist visas because even Washington D.C. knows they'd stay and get jobs, joining the army of exploited, undocumented workers. Ali planned to go legally, as a teacher of English as a second language to fellow immigrants in his, "America, The States?"

We decided on San Francisco for him, with its mild climate, cultural mishmash, high salaries and prices, and effective affirmative action. He was learning Survival Spanglish for the Mission District ("Wha fuckin putón aquí robó mi fuckin jacketa pues?!")

La Mission, ¡Donde Está La Acción Locochón! which Khalid picked up as a cheer he'd lead his fellow TV'ers in, during our sleepy afternoon apartment hunts in slow beach cafes. Pues la onda es todo universo Eses.

Ambitious Ali had joined the summer trek of street vendors selling everything, north from Fes to tourist-rich Tanger, and for the beach — summers are killers in the South, they say. He sold cigarettes from a wide wicker basket, a mound of dried squash seeds on the bottom forming a pedestal for his advertising sign, a red and white Marlboro fliptop box with the Philip Morris Royal Seal — two golden horses standing, their forelegs holding a golden banner proclaiming, "Veni Vidi Vici." They sure did; old Phil Morris was more successful than my poor Roman soldiers ever were.

Ali said he came to sell in Tanger because he'd be too ashamed to be seen vending cigarettes on the streets in Fes, for he was the only university student who was a street vendor. So touching, even if it was probably sweet pony turds.

I said (with dictionary) the thing I'd be most ashamed of would be eating other people if I weren't starving, and sure they were really dead. Sweet Ali said his greatest shame would be disgracing his family; I think mine was more realistic.

126

So I got to hang out along the night Boulevard with funny non-Spanish speaking Fes plastic-patch sidewalk vendors, helping them sell clothes, watches, shoes, you-name-it to the few English and Spanish speaking tourists left in September.

Ali said he was earning only about 50 dirham a day now and his cheap shared hotel room cost 25, so it was almost time to return to Fes U for the fall semester starting in October, sob. But he'd come visit me to continue our total immersion Spanglish lessons; he got ponyride lingo down quick!

Innocent Ali was not a TV service person because he'd be expelled from his university if caught by police; they even hassled the regular street vendors sometimes, or he'd have to pay them a 3,000 dirham bribe to go free. Healthy Ali smoked neither Marlboros nor anything else, but we would go to our corner window table in the Pilo Bar for lunch.

With our first 10 dirham cervezas Speciales, we each got a tiny bowl of baked beans, a silver saucer of green, brown and black olives, and a miniature tomato onion salad in oil and spices, with baby silverware – like yuppie grazing. I was eating almost everything now, on moderate Immodium diet.

With our second Speciale came a six inch fried fish apiece, which Moroccans sensibly ate with their fingers, wadding the small napkins into balls and dropping them on the frequently-swept floor. Clean restroom, friendly all Marhueco businessman place, 40 dirham plus 5 dirham tip for lunch for two in a pleasant atmosphere with Arabic music thundering out of large speakers, so many classical instruments it sometimes sounded like a European symphony. And a buzz on for our afternoon hamman exercise.

Sweet Ali vended only nights; days were for the beach and me. When I went into work, it was a peaceful escape from real life, but Liz didn't keep track of me and neither did I. She sat up in her office staring at papers on her desk or at the computer terminal, at the same thing. A classical sign of depression — I'd have to have a talk with her, a little Saliva-San Francisco therapy.

Khalid saw Sweet Ali and me lovey-dovey on Le Boulevard one morning about noon. Tanger's small, you always run into everyone, for better or worse. Worse aimed some antagonistic Arabic at my pony boy, who bared large teeth and brayed back – people just don't back down here, initially anyway.

I jumped in, in español, "Oh fuck off, Khalid, I don't need your protection anymore. You're just afraid sweet Fes boy is going to fuck me out of all your dirham!"

Sweet Fes boy didn't understand my Spanish but his bared teeth relaxed into a delicious overbite grin. Passing pedestrians on Le Boulevard were smiling, too; Khalid and I always put on an entertaining show that reached the back balconies effortlessly.

Enraged Khalid jerking at me, anchored to my solid pony, "No no, you never say that, my soon dead wife! Por Dios you never disgrace Honest Khalid on my Boulevard Tangerino! Better A Man Kill Me Than Say Bad Things Of Me!"

Disgusted, leading my pony away, "Oh that's real intelligent my deadheadest husband. You're the stupidest person I ever met, no wonder you're so impressed with me. Try a little Americano philosophy, 'Sticks and Stones May Break My Bones, But the Sweetest Words Are, Chiao Asshole!' "

Khalid babbled angry Spanabic, waggling his hands tragically in front of his face. My parting shot, "Shut up, you crazy fuckin' wop!" as Sweet Ali and I kicked up our heels and laughed all the way to our afternoon pony ride at the hamman.

Naturally, Khalid was at Abdullah's when I came home

later (whoops, so busy I forgot to go to work today, oh well, Dizzy Liz won't notice).

Los tres amigos sitting on Abdullah's and my bed, talking kif shit. First punch, "Por Dios you never listen to best worried-sick fuckybuddy Khalid, no no, you just do what you want, fuck the every puto on Le Boulevard, they steal your every dollar Por Dios!"

My face in his Levied lap, addressing his intelligence, "Oh Ali, sweet Fes baby, what happened to your palón (big stick)? It seems to have shrunk into a palito (little stick) today!"

Khalid painfully jerked my hair to face to face, lying on top of me, Abdullah laugh-shifting to protect his band-aided belly.

His spit perfumey kif, I kissed his angry tongue, "Wait Por Dios! My highest educated wife choose her puto boy by his banana and pretty face. Don't you know pretty cockface make own rule! Then thieve your everything and mine too!"

Laughing Abdullah joined the fully-clothed comedy porn show, sliding a long hand between our angry hardnesses. Abdullah didn't care about Ali and me. Once when we were Pierreing in Spanglish in our room, Abdullah congratulated me on my intelligent-for-once choice, and thanked Ali for getting his blabby wife out of his hair and face for a few hours a day.

Sometimes Abdullah could be too understanding. He was most interested in our total immersion Spanglish – the Mission District sounded good to him, too. (Of course, Khalid was already living there. Or he might move in with Saliva folks, he hadn't decided yet.)

Aroused Levi's grinding counterfeit Benetton shorts, "Por Dios, just why you think those Fes boys come up to Tanger for anyway?"

Benettons grinding back with moaning effect; thoughtfully, "To rape and pillage innocent Californianos, who never listen to their generous, most threatened benefactor, Honest Khalid."

Howling Abdullah banged into the clothed Club Pierre as Khalid rolled off me disgustedly, his face close to the wall, asking it, "So how much you pay ugly Fes puto, teeth of horse, shitty ass of old she-camel?"

Benetton bulge banging Levied butt, Abdullah ditto against me; three a squeeze on wide twin bed, "I don't pay Ali a fucking dirham, he never asks me for anything, nada, nunca."

Khalid's body whirled from the wall, wide black eyes checking mine, "But you pay the everything for him — meal, beer, hamman — yes I know the everywhere you go, the everything you do, I Tangerino!"

Quick to choking sobs, "Por Dios how could you disgrace our sacred Honeymoon Hamman with thieving Fes cigarette boy, my most whoring wife? Now everyone laugh at Khalid the cuckold, can't walk down his own Boulevard Por Dios!"

Licking his face tears, "Our honeymoon disgrace was in the fucking coche abandonada! Why can't you damn men ever get the romantic details straight?!" Khalid confused. "Sure I pay for everything, poor Ali's only making about 50 dirham a day now."

Laugh-bumping my crotch, back on familiar ground, "Hah, another lie from Fes make you pay for everything puto boy. He makes 150-200 a day plus all he can steal from you!"

Confusing Pierre positions lost our clothes, but didn't silence combatants panting across Abdullah's eager young backfield with fuzzy black center. Hissing, "And Ali takes me to interesting places, not all your boring low TV cafes, no no, we went to the Public Library to look at picture books of Fes and Old Tanger."

Kneeling between Abdullah's spreading, pleading cheeks, gasp in, Khalid leaned down towards my face between them, checking that the Trojanenz was secure and blessing their union with my mouth, "You know that is a lie, my clumsiest wife!"

Hastily uncoupling their union, twisting howling caboose onto the floor and taking its place on the Holy Abdullah Line, "Well, we're *gonna* go to the Library, that's the same fuckin' thing, don't be so goddamn linear!"

Proud Khalid back in the middle, "Hah! I Tangerino man, sell el chocolate (slang for TV), we let Fes boys sell only cigarette!"

Rude Pierre the Pig grunts and squeals drowned out the rest of the debate, but Sweet Ali, ponying at the beach, won again.

HAPPY BIRTHDAY, MOHAMMED

Whew, what a long afternoon sweatwalk, filled with wonderful Tangerino memories − as los tres amigos climbed the last steep footpath to Sueád's perfect sublet for me. High in the Medina, up near the Kasabah, the white Moorish fortress now a museum on a breath-taking rock cliff above the blue rocking Mediterranean, and dull-colored flat roofs of the Medina stairstepping down to Tanger Bay. Perfect sublet getting perfecter.

We crossed a small plaza with real kids hanging out; I liked the raucous joking one with his black L.A. Raiders cap on backwards, simón, La Missión.

Ah, a grocery store, only as wide as its doubledoors propped open with wooden crates of vegetables and fruit. Inside, surely a friendly Arabic-French-Spanish speaking grocer, who took your order from behind his door-wide counter, then gathered everything up for you − the latest in convenience stores. Sure beat the shit out of stumbling around the 7-11 at 3 a.m., trying to capture a rolling can of green chile clam dip.

A left past a yellow stucco elementary school with Mickey, Minnie, Donald, Daisy, and even Porky(!) dancing and playing a violin, painted on the front, kids outside futilely shooting marbles on the grooved step street.

Then left again down a meter-wide cul-du-sac − oh goddesses, how would I ever find my way back here? Pues, putón Khalid had probably already moved in, despite our long serious kif discussions about what being a True Fucky Buddy really meant. He agreed with it all, except the no-money part and not living with me. Worthless Abdullah laughed at us; he never helped me make Khalid be more responsible, only resorting to low camel epithets ("Imperialist lacky puto camel cum in own shithole," ad nauseam).

132

Along my perfect short cul-du-sac, the houses joined on top of each other; they were actually a beautifully peeling pastel two- and three-story stucco wall with small windows and wooden doors, all open, a good sign.

In the doorway of the taller, freshly white-painted house at the end of the cul-du-sac, stood a plump smiling old woman in a red and white striped Berber skirt. In her fast Spanish-French-Arabic-Berber(?) she clasped my hand and introduced herself as Susana, my new mother(?) as translated by mocking Abdullah, her face and hands so emotional and expressive, Ana Magnani, my new landlady?

Fuck Ana Magnani, I dragged Abdullah aside; Khalid was already bragging with gestures to his new Berber mother in Arabic about He-Honest Khalid, Me-Oldest Friend. I'd heard it so often I knew it by heart even though I didn't understand a word. The way his new Berber mom studied loud Khalid, her wary gray eyes growing hard, made me suspect she was at least of average intelligence.

Low frantic Missión, "¡Chingóname Ese! What is this New Mother shit? Even a new Berber mother would be two too many – please, with my life I need anonymity, a fucking *cave* in la Medina!"

Giggling Abdullah, "Shh, locochón. Don't disgrace yourself in front of your new camel neighbors. Señora Susana lives on the first two floors, on the third floor a couple of camelrooms for storage, and you live on top, on fourth floor – baby she-camel finally on top!"

Low, "I shit your chingado camel jokes out your mother's hairy asshole! Listen, shithead, I'm gonna be draggin' every fuckin' puto in the Medina in here drunk and crazy all hours of the night with TV smoke everywhere. I mean is Berber mother gonna ground me, or stick her jeweled shafra up my blond treasure box or what?!"

Abdullah's graceful slim fingers lightly around my neck, "Shut the fuck up, locochón – you want an apartment or do you want to listen to Khalid's tired cameldung in cafes

133

the rest of your highly unnatural life?"

His fingers loosening; weakly, "But–but Abdullah!"

His perfect hands cupping my blubbering baby face, his eyes gentler, stronger than mine, his español slower and sweeter, "Trust me, my only lovewife of my miserable camel life. You will be very quiet and polite to Señora Susana, and very quiet but friendly to your neighbors on the street, for this is a family neighborhood, not like my squalid camel shack. Be sure to close the shutters and windows when you fuck, play rock music, you know the routine."

Child, "Yah, just like in the Mission."

Face squeeze, "Our future home, ese. And la Señora Susana will be stoic she-camel with your TV putos – as long as you escort them up her first three floors – these old widows have lots of stuff, never throw anything away, and are suspicious of thieves like your friends."

How could I argue with that? Hands now at our sides so not to disgrace the neighbors who were surely watching us from narrow windows and flat roofs. "Thanks, Perfect Abdullah, you always make me feel better. I only pray that's not just more gelding shit you're feeding me to calm my ass down, Incháallah!"

Abdullah affectionately twisted my camel ear to Khalid in the doorway, already Arabic-arguing with his Ana Magnani mother, who was outshouting him with ease. I admired her flouncy pajama-print pantaloons, jodhpurs(?) for Berbers were proud horse people, under her long red and white striped killum skirt that didn't meet in the front, allowing for easy movement, to leap on a horse?

White skinned, light-eyed North African Berbers have been invaded by Romans, Arabs, Portugese, French, Spanish, plus each other. But they say the proud Berbers were never conquered inside, though today most of them are farmers with pitifully small plots of land where they grow veggies, fruit, herbs, and small animals to sell in the market or to stores and restaurants. Berber women on foot make their sales rounds with large folding baskets of produce, in their bright striped skirts, hair covered with a white wrap and maybe a floppy straw hat.

Skepticism about my new Berber mom turned to Moorish intrigue as Khalid led me speeding up the narrow curling stair tunnel that was so fucking low that I banged my head twice, no blood, only matching sparrow eggs on my stunned forehead. Khalid embarrassing me, laugh-fussing over my silly new eggs as we reached the top of the Hobbitt tunnel, which opened directly into my fourth floor living room.

I pushed him away with a low "Tabone Deemak!" for there sitting on a gray and purple striped killumed divan was my only successful rental agent. Perfect nurse Sueád smiling in her perfect L.A. karate instructor's outfit: purple tie dyed jeans with matching baggy t-shirt, frizzy short hair, light blusher with violet lip gloss and purple painted toenails in sandals I wanted to kneel before, kiss, and suck.

Instead, "¡Hola, Sueád! L'bas pues," a faithful chest slap for my sublet queen.

Sueád politely laughed perfect small teeth, and in cultured español told me to look around. Yes! Empty white built-in shelves above killumed divans along three walls of the white living room, so tiny that Khalid and I were already elbowing for possession. Camel-commenting Abdullah sat down, not next to Sueád, I noted; heavy Berber Granny(?) still huffing up the Hobbitt tunnel.

Khalid and I pushed each other into my other postage stamp white room which overlooked the street, two small windows with their dark wooden shutters open to the breeze and a view down the narrow window-walled cul-du-sac, then another window-wall at the end and clear afternoon sky. So quiet, no traffic sounds for there was no traffic; I could hear neighbors' voices clearly in houses with their doors and windows open. Abdullah was right, of course, about buttoning up the old bedroom before buckerooing.

A heaven-blue killumed double bed with Khalid clowning on it already occupied half the room; the other half was a fully equipped, one-person kitchenette. Plus a low table under the window between the kitchenette and bed — cushion sitting time again, just like my old Berkeley hippie days back in the late 70's.

Next to the wee kitchenette were tiled yellow and black dwarf steps tunneling up to my terrazza, the walled, flat roof used for clothes lines, TV antennas, eating and hot night sleeping. Or lolling away hot afternoons sitting on cushioned killums under shady sunscreen TV, munching olives of many colors, agua Sidi Ali, and the large size glass bottle of Coca Cola on a silver tray, laugh-scoffing the inevitable water droplets in perfect crystal goblets — Real Mediterranean Life, another dream fantasy come true, Hámdullah!

"Holy Fuck!" Even Suéad and Berber granny laughed nervously as I swooned my first view from the rooftop terrazza. So high, flying above — on the right, downtown Tanger, white, lowrise, climbing its hill from the bay, like old pics of SF before Big Money Manhattanized the downtown, gee thanks, Joe Alioto and Dianne Feinstein.

In front, quiet so-blue Tanger Bay, beach and two docks, few ships. By leaning over the low white adobe wall on the extreme left corner of the flat roof, I could see a slice of the Holy Mediterranean and vague dark outlines of the coastal mountains of Anadalusia, Spain, fogged-in again.

Racing across rooftops, pursuing being pursued, Cary Grant in "To Catch a Thief," hopscotching flat roofs from the Kasabah down to Tanger Bay, vaulting over narrow footpaths, jellaba'ed brown faces awed up at me. Then cool moon Tanger night terrazza true love — a Real Tangerino Fantasy!

136

". . . months sublet, and I hope that price is all right for you," said Sueád seriously.

Whirling, catching my neck on a pesky clothes line, bouncing back, "Ha, I bet clothes dry really fast up here," gingerly fingering the empty metal line. "Uh, I'm sorry, Sueád, I was so admiring my new view I kinda spaced out there for a minute. What did you say?"

Khalid and Anna Magnani were Arabic out-emoting each other on my suddenly too small terrazza, 15′ x 15′(?), Abdullah's elbows on the wall, staring at the quiet bay, probably watching tiny camels in bikinis on the wide sand beach and inventing cruel epithets about them.

Facing me across the empty clothes line, Sueád's dark, narrow eyes so patient, her nurse's voice so soothing. Oh, goddesses! please don't let her think I'm just another rich Americano faggot doper degenerate exploiting her shiftless Tangerino boys. For they really were boys, funny, adventurous and so dependent, like Abdullah. Hmmm — strange that she and moody Abdullah barely talked or looked at each other today, hah, a little lovers' spat? Oh, goddesses! don't let her be jealous of me, but if she hated me why did she find my perfect sublet with kitchenette, where's the bathroom anyway?

". . . months. And I don't think that's terribly too much for you to pay, do you?" Sueád repeated seriously.

Oh no, fucked again! How much could "terribly too much" be? But this time, blitzing clothes line neck-tackled me, flipping me right onto my hard terrazza.

Sueád the nurse rescued me while sadistic camels slapped humps and bared their teeth gleeing — was this how new Berber mothers reacted in medical emergencies? Ass OK, my strongest part; neck blissfully numb, I bounced to my feet — after determining precise coordinates of the three deadly clothes lines, disguised with no clothes on.

I bet Cary Grant had stuntpersons even for chickenshit like clotheslines. Cary and Grace Kelly certainly didn't do

137

it on the set either, judging by several curious brown faces looking down on us from their privileged rooftop positions between me and the Kasabah. Tangerino terrazza fuckdream shattered, Incháallah.

While illbred camels replayed meaningless mishap in rollicking Arabic, Sueád's eyes approached, narrowed with dark concern, "You surely seem to fall down and hit your head a lot. Are you sure you should be here?"

Español perfect for melodrama, "Ah, my sweet Sueád, you're quite the perceptive psychologist, for an L.A. karate instructor."

Narrowed eyes black-hated me, then quickly blinked to angry, "Stuff your stupid fucking jokes, you're worse than Abdullah! And why don't you make him stop his childish, insulting camel obsessions?"

Housebreak my camel or camelbreak my house? And "worse than Abdullah?" Oh no, was I losing perfect sublet of unknown price to hissy catfight, handicapped by an already swelling throat? But Sueád was right about his camel obsession. Restless Abdullah was bored smoking kif and staring at his books all day, until Khalid and I dragged him to a cafe or a funny movie, like Jackie Chan dubbed in French. He'd be better off in stimulating Paris, and I might live off him there after I got bored here, or fired from my job for forgetting it existed.

Español be loud and distracting in sublet emergencies! "Oh Sueád, my head is my strongest part!" fake-rubbing it while telegraphing a tender look for support from Fair Abdullah, now slouching against the wall. "Abdullah can tell you how strong my Kansaño farmer body is."

Growling as he stalked to the other side of our ex-terrazza, "How would I know anything about your scrawny Kansaño camel she-body, chingado putón locochón, tabone deemak pues!"

Oh perfect sublet terrazza nightmare! Five seconds to breathe-decide the rest of my life, help me Khrishnamurti

– no fear, booming, "¡Es Perfecto! Exactly what I wanted, Sueád, mi amigaza!"

Brisk business Spanish to regain my sanity, my hand on her bare, hairless arm, she withdrew it, "And tell me, does la Señora Susana require a deposit, first and last months' rent, cleaning fee, key fee, bribe or anything else?" listening closely for dirham clues.

They all laughed and I learned nothing. Oh, well, Abdullah was rich, and Khalid could hustle more dumb tourists. My kinda-family squeezed single-file back down the terrazza steps, through bedroom-kitchenette to fill the three divans in my 10′ x 10′(?) sitting room, deal-sealing time, be cool.

On a small round table seeped granny's dynamite-smelling mint tea, in a silver pot with droppy glasses. With dignity, she poured a sample in the bottom of her glass, swirled it, smelled it, then slurped it, pronouncing it fit to drink, then pouring for all with delicate filips of her thick, pale wrists.

La Señora Susana was speaking her loud, highly expressive Arabic-Berber-French-Spanish from which I fished an individual word every sentence or two. It sounded like Spanish but it just wasn't – I'd be going along nodding my head, "Sí, sí," then realizing I didn't have the foggiest; she might be telling me the rent was 1,000 dirham (unlikely), or 3,000, god help me!

Abdullah and Khalid no help, camel swapping insults on their divan. Sueád softly told me it was time to fork over the 3,000 dirham. Oh god, for how long – pray for the first and last month rule, for 3,000 per month would be half my $660 salary, minus a 20% withholding income tax, Liz said?

Purring new Berber mom promised through Sueád to wash and iron my clothes, feed me sometimes, and clean my apartment once a week. Were her services included in mystery rent? What the fuck, friendly Americanos are

139

beloved around the world for being generous tippers. Besides, I insisted on making my bed and washing my own dishes, Americano male customs my Berber granny found vastly amusing but finally acquiesced to.

My new manager? landlady? body guard? Sra. Susana and I closed the deal with a firm, confident handshake, her wide gray eyes set off handsomely by her deep blue tattoos. A blue cross was tattooed on her forehead between her eyes and blue designs ran in a line from her lower lip down her chin and neck.

No lying papers, just a handshake and a smile – how we farmers did business together, from Saliva, Kansas to the Rif Mountains of Morocco, translated Sueád skeptically.

Back down the head-ducking stairs, trying to peek in the rooms on the three floors going down, doors all closed, good, I liked privacy. Spilling out the doorway at the end of my perfect cul-du-sac, congratulatory goodbyes and relieved promises to return mañana misma! with all my shit in a suitcase and black plastic grab-bags now living in the corner of Abdullah's dark cell that made my perfect sublet with kitchenette bloom like a luxury Las Vegas camel brothel!

Abdullah later told me the skinny on the rent, after we'd kicked Khalid out for the night; Abdullah's small room couldn't tolerate long periods of Khalid's restless rambunctiousness. Abdullah teased me, of course, about members of the Exploiting Class not having to fret their pretty heads with bothersome details, like how much things cost. I agreed for him but not for me.

Perfect sublet it would be: for nine months, while Sueád's alleged girl friend studied in Barcelona; the rent, 1,500 dirham a month, the 3,000 was for the first two months, whew; and Señora Susana's maid services were extra. Such an experienced, hefty she-camel should be worth an extra 100 dirham a month, opined Abdullah.

I slapped him for that, and for the tacky Kansaño camel

remark on the terrazza, too. The only problem was that Abdullah enjoyed being sharply thrill-slapped as a surprise occasionally, but I wouldn't let him slap me back, that was Khalid's job – and his Puto's Union might get my visa revoked.

And now I wouldn't have to run around Tanger every day with 4,000 dirham in my careful pocket. Chinese knew cash the best way to close a deal quick and bargain the price down – an opportunity not taken advantage of in the perfect sublet case because the price was not known, and prospective tenant was too rattled to fake terrazza amnesia.

Oh well, at least Liz would be happy now I'd be coming into work every day, and we could have our little chat about her depressed state. But 35 hours a week? A ver, maybe I could take advantage of depressed state, in a mutually beneficial way, of course.

But stubborn Abdullah refused to apologize for terrazza camel insult, reminding me that we were not prancing hand-in-hand down Castro Street. Here, he patiently lectured, one did not flaunt one's gay lovers in front of strangers who knew one, or they would ridicule one to others thus disgracing one's family and oneself. Ah, muy Latino, I explained to him, and also, on my behalf, the Dan White Twinkie temporary-insanity defense. Which he knew about, but not all the fascinating details I invented, making my Real Abdullah forget all about camel images for awhile. ¡Gracias por todo, amigaza Sueád!

Of course my perfect sublet never was. I moved in the weekend of Mohammed's birthday in September, with groups of young men chanting praises to him and to Allah through the night streets, though my plazita convenience store stayed open till its usual 11:30 p.m.

And fantastic holiday granny food, cous-cous poulet, tangine fish stew, thick harira soup, fresh goat cheese, grapes, dates, figs — ladit! ("delicious" in Arabic) Kind of like Xmas without murdering pine trees and orgying through the malls.

But all my visitors didn't want to leave — ever. Neighbors, relatives, kids, friends, all holiday visiting to scope out the new nigger in the hood up in his moving-in littered crib (no horn). But mostly they talked Arabic for hours on end with beaming new Berber mother smiling proudly, when she wasn't squabbling with Khalid. He'd already ordered me to order vicious senile she-camel out of our own private digs. I instructed him in correct singular pronoun usage, even if they were actually possessive adjectives, but he didn't catch it.

After enough mint tea again to float a mighty Mustapha he-camel, and more fractured sometimes-no-español twitching conversation, I'd have my own Mohammed's happy birthday party sprawling on my hard but wide double bed, watching my new-old blue killum glow under my ass while reading books about Morocco from the American Library, Hámdullah! In my usual shorts, no shirt no shoes, it was too damned hot, so what if King Hassan himself climbed four floors to check out the latest gringo; he already knew all about me anyway.

Through my plazita, with its small killum shop to serve them, moved groups of guided white tourists, many of them senior citizens in Tempe golfwear, descending stone footpaths from the Kasabah museum to shopping below on the Medina's main bazaar lanes, like my Lion Street where the merchants naturally paid the guides for bringing them there.

But I was the only gringo living in the immediate neighborhood, though Barbara Hutton's villa, for sale they said, was below my own villacitita, fast becoming much too chiquititita!

"What the fuck I gotta do to get my disappeared anonymity back, move to putón Nueva York?!" I yelled at

Abdullah when some cosmic miracle found us alone together for a few seconds. We were tacking up posters he was lending me of Janis Joplin and Jimi Hendrix, and the Moroccan National Football (soccer) Team in living, hairy muscle legs color. Madonna and Marlon better left at Abdullah's where they could protect him, for they'd gotten my ass outta there quick that scarlet tickle night.

Fuck! These walls sure were hard and the pushpins, wisely brought in a baggie from SF, kept slipsliding out of my hot red fingers in my fourth floor walkup head-banger minifuckingsweatbox!

I hurled the push-pins at littered grab-divans, and we hugged in excessively furnished kitchenette, hiding our naturalness from all the curious camel eyes, as rude Abdullah called them, peeking up the stairs right into my minature sitting room, no door. A colorful Liz killum would be hanging there pronto after the holidays, and I would teach them the polite Americano custom of knocking on the killum. Or at least announcing one's presence before direct eyeshot from the top of the stairs through bedroom doorway (also doorless, that made two killums hanging, and counting), eyes directly on my blue-killumed zoo world double bed.

Oh well, if camels were curious dumb enough to barge in while I was doing my deliciousness, that was their problem. My heart may be in Marhuecos, but me bed's in San Pancho Siempre (always).

Our sweaty rocking-hugging banged furnished pots, pans, and dishes in my kitchenette built for one (why do people keep so much shit they never use?). Groaning piteous español, "Oh Perfect Abdullah, you gotta help me! At least in Nueva York they'd murder me quick and viciously, instead of boring me to death with kindness — killing my spirit just like Saliva! And some of them don't even speak Spanish, like my landlady — and she talks so much in I don't know what language on her 100 trips a day up that goddamn terrazza trail right through my bedroom-kitchenette! Fuck Sueád's perfect sublet!" wailing in his thick black kinks. We were the same height and slim build so we fit perfectly, if briefly, in all our lives.

Cynical Abdullah chuckle, "Haughty she-camel Sueád make good cook." Throwing up his arms to protect his face, "Don't hit me, I'm expecting it!"

"I'm too pissed to hit."

Perfect Abdullah's hard body and soft words overflowed the relieved kitchenette as he led me to sit beside him on the bed, arms around, heads together, fuck curious camel eyes.

"Calm down, locochón. The magic word here is 'descansar' (to rest). It's a euphemism for everything. Tell fierce Berber mother you need to descansar, and she'll stay downstairs for a couple of hours and shoo Khalid and the other camels' curious noses from under our perfect lovetent."

By the time my only husbandwife Abdullah raced back up four corkscrew flights after informing mom of our extreme need for rest, my shorts were on the floor and four wooden shutters and two windows were closed in Our Bedroom (fuck the kitchenette) to sullen afternoon bay whisps, and proud loud rooster crows.

Pobre gallo, probably for Mohammed's feast, imprisoned a roof down, his leg tied to a shady post with water and a short cord. "Puc-puc-puc-puhdoodle!" his girl friend just laid an egg on an adjoining roof. She got to live and was making sure everyone remembered. I loved their scat music; sometimes the disoriented rooster crowed all night. I wanted to Cary Grant down there and liberate them, but where would a nervous escaped chicken couple go in Tanger? I'd have to eat them; it was all too complicated, plus I wasn't even a citizen yet.

Rocking to Radio Madrid, hard perfects took necessary but painful precoital piss – so much Sidi Ali and inevitable mint tea — in my new 15 dirham "taza," a pink plastic chamber pot. For the little concrete feet and cold water only showerhead high above them, were down in Sudamérica on the first floor. Next time, I'll be sure to ask, if clothes lines don't get in my way.

I admonished laughing grabbing Love Of My Lives that I certainly was not the type to piss in my own kitchenette sink, and I didn't want his rancid camel piss in there either. Our descanso lasted 14 hours, until our taza runneth over, but lucky us, we had an understanding grandmother.

SHARK BITE

But a natural Irish law that when life is all together swimming, easing the nightmare of daily existence, with hope glimmering of an only semi-violent death some distant day — Shark Pops Up.

My shark was a letter from my best Nueva York fuckbuddy, smart, funny, opinionated, outspoken — great fun for a day and a night.

Yes, I had checked into Dawson y Dawson Exports early the next morning at 11 and moody Liz shrugged at a fat letter for me in a stack of mail; it was well towards the bottom, whoops.

Mail from home, yippie! And from my wittiest correspondent, too! I rushed down to my basement killum cave, flopped on my blackgold inspection table (dusty?), and in all alone anticipation, breathed:

Lower East Slums
Nueva York
9-21-91

Dear Who In The Fuck Do You Think You Are Superstar?

Not even a hackneyed picture postcard from you yet, you rotten cocksucker, and you are. Just because you're probably deluged with fan mail from the States, Latin America, and Asia? My congrats too and a review later of your spectacular debut.

But first, your new life in Morocco: I hope you're not encountering too much frightening hostility due to the recent war of King George the Reborn Macho, and that people will come up and talk to you on the streets without too much anti-imperialistic invective. Or are you pretending to be Canadian again, ay? Or does that help anymore?

Oh well, I guess I shouldn't worry too much about your being stoned to death by the inevitable anti-American mobs, you're so charming and friendly and such a slut you've probably got those darling Moroccan men (so I've heard) eating out of your dorky Hanes already.

But I assume you're exercising discretion in the dong department, after our serious discussion in bed the last time you were here, about the perils of excessive promiscuity in these dark plague days, i.e., I hope your gross of spermicided Trojanenz hasn't run out yet.

Law school continues to be interesting and boring, and Nueva York continues to disintegrate; it's the only place to live, except maybe Paris (as you know, Frisco's too provincial, a Kansas that gets laid).

But I know you're just dying to hear about You-You-You, typical youngest child who never grew up, and how your new porn-stardom is being received by the Whores of Babylon in Manhattan. My fuckbuddy Daniel, whom I'm sure you remember from Gil and Roger's dinner party in Brooklyn Heights when you were here in August (they had to throw that nice lace tablecloth away, shame on you!). Well, Daniel brought me over your first starring video, "Saddam Meats California Pussy Boy," that he'd picked up at his neighborhood porny store — he collects Third World cock videos. Imagine our surprise, you tricky little whore, not telling us!

I assume you did not choose the title, although it's hilariously dumb enough to be yours. We howled all the way through it and even whacked each other off during the artistic asswork scenes. You lucky, lucky baby, your fat white freckled ass was never better covered. Our sperm, however, was aimed breathlessly at The Star, what a Fuckin' Horse!!

I mean in every way; did they have to use a stunt anus for the climax scene? I guess not, your vast experience the best stretcher. Remember, I had to wear chains to keep from falling all the way in last month!

Saddam, a hot topical pseudonym, I presume, delivered his hilariously dirty lines with such seriousness, a great natural comedian! Like, "I, Saddam Hussein, explode my big Scud missile in you, George. No, you too ugly, you be Barbara." Or, "I Desert Storm your tiny white Schwarzkopf!" He could be the next gay Gracie Allen!

We could discern your corncob Kansan hand in the script, like, "My Golden Fleece Treasurechest Surfbitch," that had to be you. I hope you're close, close friends off the screen as well; imagine being ravaged by him every night, ah, after growing up in Saliva with Huck Finn the macho dude of your wet daydreams.

Everyone here (except Gil and Roger) is planning to troop over to Tangiers to sponge off you over Xmas. We'd like to order one delicious, toasted Saddam to come in your bed while you're at work earning our cous-cous.

But were your lines dubbed? Your voice sounded strange, sort of garbled. And I hope even you wouldn't be so trite to resort to old saws like, "Let me throw that monster over my shoulder and burp it!" Unless they paid you mucho; are you getting a percentage of the gross? Do you have an agent yet? Try to get full script approval next time; maybe you can collaborate with your love clown Saddam. And what happened to your eye? Or was that just a prop suggesting S&M?

I'm sure you remember that Daniel (your water-goblet Chivas drinking buddy before you jumped on the table to scream the Guatemalan(?) National Anthem) has been taking some Third World classes at The New School. He's going to show "Saddam Meats California Pussy Boy" to his Intercultural Personal Relationships Seminar, as a "humorous, psychosexual metaphor on post-colonial First-Third World relationships."

I'll let you figure it out; all pretty obvious, with the topper being the Third World's forceful rejection of bandaged, half-blind First World's pathetic attempts to penetrate and ravish Third World's untouched primitive depths, etc., etc. You played that scene so realistically, my dear, but surely you're plugging Saddam's hung buns regularly, lucky Saliva kid wins again!

But for me, it was just a hot home-jerkoff video, made funny by having fucked the supporting actor, a first for me! Will you autograph my erection next time through?

Now don't go getting your dumb Irish up, because the following criticism is meant to be sincerely constructive: don't quit your day job.

Sure, you were your usual crazy fuckself, and tragi-comic getting slapped around by our fearless Moroccan hero when you were trying to rape his great hairy ass (like Lucy trying to rim surly Ethel, who for once was not going along), I'm getting hard.

Please rush me grosses of colored nude glossies, signed "Suck on This. Love, Saddam." Thanks, kiddo.

But you, my most entertaining bouncing-off-the-coast companion for life, you have not the requisite hard nor soft good looks, nor the essential X-rated

149

equipment, to do porn as more than an occasional whim. (There aren't many blond, blue-eyed American exhibitionists there, right?)

Please tell sweet Saddam that everyone in Nueva York (except Gil and Roger who refused to watch it) tells him he can write his own ticket to Hollywood Porn Stardom, gay or straight or just jerking his very hairy bozooka onto the camera lens with his cannonballs dragging, I'm getting harder.

But beneath his muscled, rough exterior, he showed a tenderness and humor, symbols of the Third World's tenacious survival instincts, according to tiresome Daniel.

I agreed, however, with Daniel about the effectiveness of using only the one camera shooting from above. So avant garde for a porn flick to make the camera an unmoving participant, waiting for Third World to drag First World back into God's omniscient eye for further humiliation (I wish Daniel would just shut up; maybe I'll stop seeing him and move back to Akron. No great loss, he's even worse in the sack than Calif. Pussboy. Ha, just half kidding.)

You might want to talk with the distributors because there seems to be a problem. When Daniel returned to the porny store to pick up copies for me and everyone you know in North and South America and all the ships at sea, the shop owner said it was sold-out and he couldn't get any more copies; there had been a mistake and "Saddam Meats" was intended exclusively for the Asian market. What's the Mafia up to now? Or maybe you were afraid your Saliva farmers might see it and all want to fuck Young Kansaño Frankenstein with their flaming pitchforks the next time you sneaked back into the Jaysquawk State?

Not to worry, little bro: of the fifty-odd copies we made (thanks to Visa), the one sent closest to Kansas went to Chicago, to Richard, the ex-priest who runs the AIDS foundation there. You probably don't remember but he was the one who tried to pull the tablecloth from under your and Daniel's tangoing feet, causing the most destructive rips when you got tangled in it, and crashed into Gil and Roger's priceless antique highboy which is now living in the repair shop. They say you're the reincarnation of Jessie James!

Quick, send me a nice Moroccan weaving to replace their dumb tablecloth and maybe they'll let me back in their apartment — I need rich food, even fuck for it sometimes.

Well, my dear boy, you've certainly lived out another fantasy for us dull stay-at-homes, speaking of which, I called your sweety confused Saliva mom to get your address. She proudly informed me that her youngest, cutest son's infrequent postcards said he had a good job with medical coverage, was appreciating the rich Moroccan culture and food, and mostly staying home at night in his cozy, quiet seaside villa, above Barbara Hutton's even, with his new Moroccan mother, studying his French and Arabic dictionaries.

I choked and dropped the phone; told your mom that a mob of hungry crack muggers had just invaded my building, so I had to hang up and move the Tomahawk missile launcher in front of my door. That'll give her some juicy gossip for Baptist Bingo Night, if that isn't a triple oxymoron.

Oh fuck, it's the midnight roach attack, where's my trusty Sony flame-thrower? 8 a.m. class tomorrow and I haven't even started to read the shit yet. But first, I must study First-Third World exploitation cum flick and squirt all over Sweetie Pie Saddam again.

And I got carried away here with you, as always, I rewrote this even, you know you're wonderful.

And please please try to at least show up at your job, don't blow another one. Write back tonight, take a break from your dictionarying — and don't forget colored autographed glossies of your magnificant Moroccan Lover, another Saliva fantasy come true!

Does your seaside villa have a rooftop pool, stocked with friendly, mocking pool boys? Hurry, build one before Xmas!

> *Forever Bicoastal Love,*
> *Edgy Rick*

P.S. Did you see Elvis fucking a camel yet? When I think about that story when the Mexican cowboy Loocky Pierre picked you up hitch-hiking on his horny she-mule —

Keep your buns saggy, you leave me laughing again, till I get to my Saddam remote control. XXXOOO! And to you too, dear boy.

Back to unreality slintering, my screaming fists, feet beating goldblack innocent-victim sacrifice pyre, inspection lights my ass!

My savage tears were confused about which was killing me more, fucking Mustapha's treachery or Edgy Rick's insulting review, that jealous asshole! I wanted to murder the both of them, the Sarcastic Messenger and his X-rated Horse!

A heavy hand on my sobbing shoulder, was it He? Was the camera all set for his fist-fucking snuff sequel, "Vicious

Saddam Hoofs PinkVirgin California Slutbitchboy?"

Screaming, I rolled over. It was only friendly Liz offering me her white lace hanky, her husky voice shaking with concern, "What the fuck's wrong with you, too much snorting alleged substances off the balcony tabletops in your cheap cafes?"

She pulled me up, god was she strong, to sit beside her ample ass spreading on goldblack porn bench. I wailed desperately into her comforting silver and black curly tangles, "My-my mother, has just di-died!" (Oh no, wrong lie, she'll make me go back to Saliva for the funeral!)

Her pudgy bare arm around me, our teary heads together, just like junior high. This would be nice to film but the inspection lights weren't on. Liz overflowing dramatic concern, "You must return to Kansas at once!"

Patting her soft shoulder to strenghten me, nice gray silk blouse with matching pants, for a little lunchy later at the old Chickie Shack Chateau? Oh no, my mom was still dead! "Uh, she's not exactly dead, actually."

Her plump body stiffened, I patted faster, "What?"

"Uh, she's just kinda dying – of pornography." (Oh no, I didn't mean to say that!)

Liz lightly to the bottom of the stairs, a safe several meters away, her narrowed violet-greys studying me. Ah ha, based on her rash reaction to my pornography slip, she was probably in on it too, with her fucking Trojanenz Horse Mustapha. Yes! Here was the perfect opportunity to discreetly interrogate suspected Evil Pornring Queen!

Friendly, neutral, "And how do you feel about pornography, Mom, I mean Liz, I mean Ms. Dawson y Dawson?!" (Oh no, I was losing it! Maybe my mom really was dead and now I would move back to sweet Saliva where I'd never have to have a real conversation again!)

Grey curious eyes, "With my hands, I guess," sitting down on the bottom step on an old piece of cardboard. "And one Dawson is quite enough, thank you. What do

153

you mean, your mother is dying of pornography?" from the relative security of her bottom step.

Deep, long sighs, scrambling brain breathing, "Uh, have you please got a cigarette by any chance, Ms. Dawson, heh?"

Sharp Liz Bitch, "Cut the stalling crap, Buster, I was married before, remember?"

Ah, but clever diversion gave me time to weave, sincerely, "Well, frankly, Ms. Dawson, you know how they are back in Kansas."

Nodding, getting into it, "Yeah, where is it y'all are from — Spermicide, KS?"

The miracle of mutual laugher, "Ha, that's a good one, Ms. Dawson! I'll have to include that in my next long letter home! It's Saliva, actually."

Liz switch to pushy mother, "Speaking of spermicide, I certainly do hope and pray, my dear boy, that you're practicing safe sex with all your sleazy boys here. I see you on the Boulevard laughing it up with every damned puto on the street!" Shrugging her fat indifferent shoulders on her step, "Oh well, you'll get ripped off, and probably still not learn your lesson."

Fake sniffing, fake fighting back real tears, blowing as much snot as I could conjure up into cruel Liz's tacky snotrag; whimpering, "Here–here my poor ma-mother's, dying of pornog-nography, all–all alone in-in Sa-Saliva!" Fast, pissed, "And all you can fucking do is lecture me like I'm some kind of immoral teenage hoodlum degenerate!" wailing some more.

Her solo booming laughter so hurtful to innocent victim, "Oh yeah, your poor ol-old ma-mother dying of Spermicide in her Saliva, why do you keep saying that, it's getting so tiresome!"

Breathing down my justifiable rage, oh goddesses, to spring Snide Porn Queen Trap, "Well — my dear Ms. Dawson, as I may have mentioned before, my highly civicly–minded mother is chief layperson at The First Church of the Rampaging Baptists of Greater Saliva, as well as chairperson emeritus of Saliva Mothers United To Stamp Smut Out Of Our Children!"

Liz looked like a stunned she-pig grunting on her small step, good. Leaning forward from the height advantage of my goldblack bench, friendly, personal, "Well, Ms. Dawson, being yourself from Mountain View, you know from your own experience what cruel bastards people in medium-sized cities can be. And well, anyway, my darn cousin Zebediah, too black–leather bookish for Saliva, took off on his motorcycle for Hollywood and Vine, had it stolen, was living on the streets with the wrong crowd, and, well, to earn a few extra bucks to feed his ravenous Kansaño food habit, poor Zebediah foolishly agreed to pose in an X-rated homosexual movie. And now all the Salivans are being vicious in their kind way, and my poor mom had her near-fatal forenoon heart attack on the kitchen floor, and fell and hit her head, no that was me, you know what I mean!" (Whew! Thanks goddesses, great except the end!)

Trap sprung on innocent victim again, hard, "You mean you're telling me that goddamned Mustapha got you too?! I'm gonna kick his fake jellaba ass!"

Stunned victim biting slippery handkerchief, "Oh, it's not fake at all, Ms. Dawson y– "

Shrill, "I mean the goddamn jellaba!" Leaning forward on her step, good cop Liz, "Where did he do it to you, honey? In a hotel? On the beach?"

Jury in, Alleged Porn Queen Acquitted pending further revelations; mumbling, "I don't know where, uh yeah, I guess, I haven't even seen it, that's what the letter was about."

Hard Liz bad cop, "Ha! I thought it was just a-little-bit-strange that someone would write you from New York that your mother was dying in Saliva. And Kansas does have telephones now, even in its Spermicides, no? You're slipping, my child."

Terminally pissed, "I'd just gotten my four page suicide note and I guess I was a little upset, you might say!"

Pissed back, "And I say using your poor dear mother in your filthy lies — that's terrible! You should be ashamed of yourself!"

Chanting, "And-if-she-dies-it-will-all-be-my-fault. Shit, I been using that excuse ever since my degenerate K.U. country club days, and she's still healthier than you or me taken apart and put back together. Which is what I'd like to do to that motherfuckin' Mustapha right now, but not put him back together!" too pissed to cry more.

Softly plopping herself back up on my bench, arm around, mother-clucking, "I know, I know, honey. I'd heard gossip about Mustapha taping unsuspecting horny blond tourists en flagante delicto. I confronted him about it, but of course he denied it with all the indignation of the obviously guilty. But I'd heard he always distributed his spontaneous sex flicks only to continents other than the victim's."

Cuddling against her fleshiness, "There was only a limited, mistaken release in the States."

Soft, "Oh that's good, honey."

Loud jerk away, "Until my asshole ex-best New York fuckbuddy here," crushing sharkbite letter into a hardball crashing like Welch, Stew or the Eck into killumed homerun wall. "He made like a jillion copies to send all over the uncivilized world! But at least not near Kansas, or so he alleges. Shit, my poor mom's probably dead on her kitchen floor right now!" sniffling into Liz's slick snotrag.

Comforting backpats, "It'll be all right dear, just you wait and see. Mustapha's an occasional good lay, if you don't let him talk and do it in the dark; he hasn't discovered infra-red cameras yet."

156

Indignant sniffling, "So that's why you keep his ugly ass around here! Why didn't you warn me?!"

Her naturally throaty laughter back; I relaxed and fished wadded hanky mío from the back pocket of my work jeans. I handed her slimy one back to her, but she let it drop to the floor. I hate it when people don't consider janitors, especially when I was the fucking janitor and everything else down in hellhole underground porn studio.

Deep Liz chuckle, "I didn't even know you knew him, socially that is. And you act so Mister Cool World, who's to warn you about anything? And are you crazy, why would I keep a pompous ass like Mustapha when there are so many beautiful, nice men here? No, Mustapha's a, how do I put this delicately – he's a, uh, fixer."

Triumphant at last! "Hah! I knew he was a cop all along!"

Deep Liz laughter continued, too-heavy backslaps began, "By the way, I was going to take you to the Chauteau Poulet to tell you this over a nice patio lunch, but– " her hand quiet on my back, thank goddesses; serious, low, "We're declaring bankruptcy. Not that it probably matters to happy-go-fucky you; I'm surprised you can even remember how to get here."

Shocked innocence, "Ms. Dawson! I'm surprised at you – you know how hectic it's been finding an apartment, moving in, all those Mohammed birthday parties – bankrupt? Fucking Bankrupt?!"

Her sad salt-and-pepper tangled nods made me tremble at my premature job loss, "But–but you can't be going bankrupt, I just started working here!" my sobs getting realer as the day wore on.

Her plump hand patting my tender back again, "For God's sake, don't blame yourself, I've been meaning to talk to you about what I, at least, consider to be your serious ego problem."

"Fuck ego! Oh what's gonna happen to me now?"

157

Resigned, "I don't know. It was the y Dawson part who was the problem; he's kind of gone over the edge since he ran off with a Mustapha-type to the New York office and I came here."

Resigned Deadmeat patting her back anyway, "Oh I'm So Sorry, Ms. Dawson. These things are always so painful and messy — straight, gay, or mixed. What are you going to do now, uh, Ms. Dawson?"

Shrugging, "Take some time off, visit my family in Mountain View — easy to get a job buying or in a shop — you know." Sighing, "I feel kind of relieved, liberated now from the impossible hassle of trying to manage a failing business." Bitterly, "Especially with that asshole y Dawson pissing everything away."

Turning to me sweetly, "And what about you, my sweet misguided baby?"

Jumping my butt down the bench away from fat, rude Liz, "I hate that shit! All my life it's been baby-this, baby-that — no wonder I'm such a misguided fucking baby!" wailing in my own damp hanky.

Maternal Liz scooted down the bench to me, arm around, patting her baby again, "Now, now, I didn't mean it that way. What will you do now?"

Sniffling, "Oh, I've got a rich lover here. Guess I'll go with him to Paris; he's gonna study there, and I could use a break."

Renewed respect in her throaty drawl, "Hey, baby, that sounds great! You're not half as crazy as I thought you were!"

Rewadding my soggy handkerchief and jamming it angrily, along with wadded pornring letter evidence, into my back pocket, I politely excused myself from slatternly Mountain View Liz, and numbly promised to come in daily early in the afternoon to prepare for the close-out sale. Then I fled up the stairs from my bankrupt porn nightmare to Perfect Abdullah's warm cave, Save Me Daddy!

APACHES ON THE WARPATH

"All I ask outta life is a little quasi-happiness and a few chucks, but they kill people for that in this world! You ga-gotta help me-me Da-Daddy!" sobbing more all over Impatient Abdullah. For once, sleepy Khalid was relieved he was not my primary husband, or gruff father.

"Shut up, locochón!" pushing my breaking heart firmly down his bed into Arabic-swearing Khalid, upsetting his kif inhalation. "Leave me the fuck alone for just one minute, locochón. I'm trying to figure out this fascinating, funny letter," again smoothing out wrinkled pornring evidence and retrieving his French-English dictionary from the floor where I'd kicked it out of his angry hand.

"I'd like to find out some more information about this New School — and this camelcat Daniel, too. He sounds like a really intelligent Americano, I didn't know they existed, and a fun putón too." Admiringly, "Did you really bust up those rich faggots' camel penthouse?"

Sullenly sitting on the bed, counting blond hairs on my tanned thighs as a peaceful retreat activity, I refused to answer under the Twinkie Dan White Amendment. Abdullah had treated my nightmare as a joke, and all insensitive Khalid had wanted to know was how he could get a starring role in my next porn flick.

Abdullah and Khalid's initial joy at the news I would be accompanying them to Paris (Khalid had invited himself along) had turned to idle curiosity about something else in Abdullah's flitty mind, while dumb Khalid was mentally packed for anywhere; maybe I should double my vitamin dosage.

Abdullah's strong lean arm around me, seductive smile, "I think we should mount our mightiest he-camels across the Atlantic River to the Lower East Side and set up our lovetents with Sidi Daniel, instead of boring Paris, locochón."

Khalid laughed joyously and tried to slap my fisted hand, then slapped and clowned with his Abdullah wit. Muy exasperated español, "Oh nothing's going right today, and you goddamn rotten camel cocksuckers are supposed to feel sorry for me, and support me in my quest for vengence against our Great Satan Mustapha. Instead, you're playing stupid Nueva York New School fantasy games, and getting fucked-up on your stupid kif," snatching the barkstick pipe from Khalid, again in his stupor, and making the eager ember pulsate angry red.

Kindly chuckling Abdullah at least slapped my manly thigh instead of pat-pat-patting my cute baby back like that cooing fruitcake Auntie Liz! I had neglected to inform my dos amigos about Mom not dying of pornography in Saliva, for why bring more derisive laughter down onto one's innocent, battered head?

"Locochón, you don't know who you're dealing with here," Abdullah's strong hand gripping my thigh and moving up to my unprotected privates. Hey, we'd just done that in our premature(?) ejaculatory celebration of Los Tres Pierres in Paris.

"Oh, no you don't, my most whorish Abdullah, you think you can get anything through our cocks!" I twisted away to sit cross-legged on the killumed floor in the narrow gap between wall and bed.

Flickering in the candlelight, the young but seasoned Apache Chief faced his courageous but wacked-out braves. Soft, commanding, "You know you must help me. You're the only ones I trust here besides Sweet Ali, but he's in Fes. I intend to call him up here for the operation."

Snorting Khalid, "Hah, Sweet Ali puto boy's operation is steal all our valuable time and money!"

Graciously ignoring the tribal half-wit, "I know that Mustapha's a cop or a fixer or both or something, I don't wanna know. So our collaborative plan, which we're working out together here in our sacred ancestral Apache

160

camel cave, must be so carefully, oh so perfectly conceived and executed."

Getting hooked in spite of themselves, their bodies and faces forward —

"Forward Ho! My mighty braves, we must design our ingenious, precise plan to meet the following objectives: Número uno: To terrorize and sexually humiliate Mr. Mustapha's delicious large asshole, as he terrorized and humiliated so many innocent blond tourist assholes!" Great laughter and hand-slaps.

"Número dos: We videotape said homosexual gang-rape humiliation in order to blackmail aforementioned felon, so that he forthwith ceases and desists aforementioned high crimes and misdemeanors, and recalls and destroys all existing copies, worldwide, of all his sexploitation video cassetes, or Betamax!" Howl-jumping camel tumult.

"Número tres! For obvious reasons, our strict anonymity must under all circumstances be strictly maintained and preserved at all costs." Heads nodding solemnly, I really had them now! ¡Mil gracias goddesses!

Casual, "Plus we can skip this boring burg for Gay Paree immediately following Operation Hobbyhorse, so what the fuck?" More raucous camelshit.

"Ahem! Número cuatro: Our soon-to-be-flaming asshole Mustapha must be lured at a precisely synchronized time to our covert humiliation film set — therein lies the fucking rub. I'll get back to you on that one pronto; we'll do lunch at the Chickie Shack."

Great hissing and derisive whistling, but I was spared the usual headbangs from my rebellious naked braves, due to my recent overdose of medical and mental emergencies in the head region. My two Tangerino husbands could indeed be sensitive, if I were half dead.

"Y El Ultimo, Número Cinco! I would like Operation Hobbyhorse to incorporate the extensive use of velcro."

Great Arabic confusion between concerned braves. My

trustworthy chief hands high, calming restless recruits with sweet firm español, "Shut the fuck up and please listen, please listen, gentlemen, and you will understand everything. I've always wanted to do a really big velcro project. And just imagine the sounds that masses of velcro ripping will make in our film! Not to mention the incredible visuals, velcroing mouths, cocks, assholes, etc. Maybe you could use it for your Masters Project at The New School, Abdullah." He nodded bewildered agreement.

"Do you know of any wholesale velcro places where we could go disguised, you know, like in rich white jellabas with those cord things around our heads, they'll think we're rich kinky Kuwaitis, and buy it in meter-wide strips?"

Excessively confused bordering on hostile Spanabic eventually quelled by steady, crossed-legs-falling-asleep Apache chief past his bedtime. "All right, all right now, calm the fuck down and chew your contented cuds and listen to your husband like the obedient she-camels I know you can be."

I finally got mighty stud braves off me after a laughing whoop attack on their playful chief on the floor; head spared again, they really cared! We sat puffing on the bed, my arm around nodding Khalid, "Khalid, my most energetic husband, it's time we got you a real job," sharply elbowing Abdullah not to laugh.

Nervous Khalid awoke, smiled, "Great!" and slapped my hand. "Only 500 dirham per day, all I need for my poor life Por Dios, plus expenses. And I don't get fucked," proudly, "for only my only wife, and baby camel zep," pinching wincing Abdullah's, "know my most secret manhood pride Por Dios!"

Shaking him, "No, no Khalid, this is not one of your usual running around tour guide jobs, copping all day for some crazy young Japanese tourist, smoking hard TV together, then eating and drinking him to death in some kickback clip joint, so you can drag him dirhamless back

162

to his hotel without having him stick his uncircumsized dick with stiff hair sticking straight out into your virgin she-camel's mouth. Oh no, my adventuresome young Apache He-Brave, this is a Real Job for a Real Marhueco Marlboro Man!"

Bored Khalid frowning, "My wordiest wife, why you have to hurt my poor brain with all your shit, go on and on and on, breaking my head Por Dios! Just cut through fucking camelshit, tell me exactly what you want me to do. Then I say no, and bargain like gentleman, but shrill she-camel insult me disgracefully and Por Dios her white eye be technicolor all over again hah!"

Accumulated frustrated fury hurled me weeping on the startled, reluctant recruit, Private Khalid, knocking him flat on the bed, sighing Abdullah rearranging himself narrowly beside us. He wasn't getting much page-staring in lately.

I was on top in an angry Irish pin, fuck Apaches, flooding Private Khalid's giggling face with tears, so easy now — all the better goddesses to Wash Out Depression Fast Fast Fast! For I'd read somewhere that the actual physical act of crying caused tears to carry depressive chemicals out of the body, so I was always careful not to cry on my cats or plants.

I did feel calmer, more organized and in control, lying on surrendering recruit getting with the program. Just a few more pieces to jiggle into place. Mail-order velcro would be too slow, Fed Ex it? They should be running the fucking government.

After heavy torture with Abdullah's and my eager stun guns in his every unholy hole, Private First Class Khalid nodding off again, pledged to accompany me to Dawson y Dawson Exports to help with all the lugging for their close-out sale. Liz would be hiring casual labor for the project, and who could be more casual than my handsome, neatly dressed, well-spoken, brave toothless Khalid?

Then we could surreptitiously set up the velcro porn

163

ring trap downstairs in the Dawson y Dawson X-entrapment studios. Lights Camera Action! Screaming Mustapha on blackgold asshole humiliation-wheel, hah!

Blackmail and vengence − this baby was acting like a real man now − as calculatingly cold and bitter mean as glaring broad-shouldered Joan Crawford herself. Fuck Softee Liz.

The next day, after sober reflection, sensible Abdullah thought Operation Hobbyhorse was harebrained, of course. "A naive foreign tourist should not play revenge games in Marhuecos, putón locochón."

I agreed, so I turned to faithful Khalid who plotted feverishly with me, trying to convert his enthusiastic loyalty into the Number One Position on my Time and Dirham Hit Parade again, fat chance.

But an all-velcro production proved to be impossible, shit, how would I ever out-Christo Christo with my velcro wall binding together all seven continents of The Earth − if I couldn't even get a few wide velcro strips here to lasso crazed outlaw killer-horse? Khalid was Por Diosing disconsolate when the only thing his associates could steal for us was a spool of long, thin velcro strips from a distributor.

All our supplies for Operation Hobbyhorse were stolen by Khalid's friends. He paid them half-price(?) for the hot goods and I paid him to pay them. It probably would have been cheaper to buy the stuff myself, but the outlaw way seemed purer, plus I didn't wanna buy that shit in any store here.

Khalid and I went camera hunting down in the basement his first day of work as Liz-peon at Dawson y Dawson Bankrupt Exports. One hundred dirham for an 8 hour day, about twice the going rate for unskilled labor here; was that why we were going bankrupt?

Oh well, I'd been a Tangerino for nearly two months

now, and it sounded like fun being a Parisiano for a minute with two of my best French-speaking fuckbuddies, and live off Abdullah's father. Abdullah told me his father approved of me because I was an educated Americano businessman and drove Abdullah to read a lot. But he didn't want to meet me; I accused his blabbermouth squealing son of telling him about my Barbary Pirate career aspirations, a charge that laughing Abdullah denied. I had him repeat the popular Americano idiom: "I am low lying sack of shit Por Dios!"

We were already eagerly planning vacations from Paris back to the Real Morocco, Sweet Ali's Fes, Marrakech, and south to the Sahara – real camels at last, but god spare us Abdullah's corny camel metaphoring; maybe *he* should be living in Saliva.

The triumph of Operation H.H. would be celebrated with champagne and more on First Class Air France to Paris; I made Abdullah show me the tickets. I in the window seat next to Abdullah, Khalid across the aisle; he was thrilled, had never flown before.

And was sworn to Honest Khalid Por Dios secrecy not to breathe a word about any of it to his jealous puto friends. Especially about the hard-to-get-for-a-young-person French tourist visa. And Khalid might just decide to live there, until we moved to La Missión Acción, pues ese.

Getting him the job was simple. Dizzy Liz, closing up home and business, trusted me again in her dire need. And smiling and cheerful, I took immediate advantage. She respected my strong Kansaño brain and back to find killums, check them off an inventory list and lug them up the basement stairs. The office equipment was gone from the killum firesale showroom, and I got to supervise the bargains lugging crew.

So I chose a couple of the desultory day laborers I'd toted and packed with, plus my landlady's poor Berber cousin in town from the Rif Mountains. He needed dirham, strong rural work ethic, and cheap.

Shy mumbling Khalid was straight out of Hee-Haw in his normal old jeans, with a worn workshirt and floppy straw hat, his dark complexion mute testimony to ruthless Moorish zeps.

Weird grey Liz look, "Yeah I guess he's okay, but no more. Use the ones we already know don't steal."

Saliva wise ass, "Pretty difficult to get something as big as a killum out with both of us here, Ms. Dawson."

Violet eyes snapping, "There are small pieces down there too. And nothing, ever, is too big to steal – get a grip on the world!"

So I grabbed my Levied zep Marhueco style for her rude horsey laughter, as she shoved me and my Por Diosing Berber cousin to the basement door with a list of shit to bring up.

10 a.m. early birds found the basement deserted except for 10 jillion fucking killums of every color, folded and waiting in heavy stacks. And my infamous inspection table with its black and gold killum about to star again, in my Cecil B. DeMille – David Lynch ass-kickin' tits-'n-sandals mini-epic: "The Proud Emir of Kuwait Welcomes Home Palestinian Expatriates to His Holiest of Holes." The film title was the only part of Op HH that haughty Abdullah approved of.

With my Berber guard posted inside the closed basement door, I wrestled a stack of killums on top of the inspection bench, then hopped up on it – Yes! In the center of the inspection lights' gridwork was a heavy black wooden box with a cleverly hidden panel on the side. It slid back to reveal a camera with Panasonic on it pointing straight down through a hole in the box that was covered with a round wood panel, Yes!

The switch activating the unseen music system and camera was under a sliding panel in a leg of the inspection

166

table; Mustapha did topnotch work, I'd have to hand it to him, my hands in him, Yes!

I figured the Mustapha part would be easy, for he'd surely come sniffing around for everything he could snatch cheap or free from poor Liz's dying business. And his ego was so perverted, I would hardly have to act.

A few days later, scavenger Mustapha swaggered in and I lured his fist stroking his shiny white tent jellaba down to a corner of the basement, behind a stack of killums. The newly promoted Berber foreperson kept the killums flowing upstairs.

Shyly tickling black hairs on horse's massive claw, "Oh, Mustapha, my favorite macho from Long Beach, after George Deukmajian, of course!"

Beaming, he guided my tiny cigarette boy's hand to help erect his jellaba tent pole and arrange it, keeping his groans discreetly low.

"Oh, Mustapha! I can't wait! I'm so glad to see you again before leaving for Paris. I was afraid I'd never have the chance to grant you your greatest Californiano Pussyboy desire!" my innocent Saliva face sunning up his dark stud features while my guilty Frisco hand jobbed his jellaba tree perfectly.

Two mastadon hooves covered my black Levied cheeks, pushing me into his jellaba limb reared upright, denting my belly to my chest. I enthusiastically dry humped his jellaba'ed tree thigh; I wouldn't have to act at all in "The Proud Emir etc." – until the last scene. But then, that might be the realest David Lynch part, Mustapha as Eraserhead from Long Beach State, Twin Peaks Leo spitting his baby cereal.

Brusque accented inglés as he imprinted my front bouncing back, "Crazy Frisco fuckhead, go to Paris with that no-spine, dangerous rich faggot boy, you don't know!" as he unzipped his trick jellaba in the middle. Heavy horse snot greased his limb filling my t-shirt, hot fucking my erect trembling chest hairs while huge horse apples rolled on my banging belly.

He politely pulled up his jellaba so my Levi's and Hanes dropped-to-knees palito could scratch between his Spanish mossed trunks. Bigger than a lot of dicks middle-finger in me so fast – thank god it felt heavily snotted – fucking my prostate so tickling quick that palito spit between mossy trunks, and mighty limb blew on gasping chest up onto my neck. My poor K.U. t-shirt was wrecked, its Jayhawk screaming joy. Or was that me?

The Berber Supervisor was shouting orders in loud Arabic with angry Spanglish interspersed, "Estupid locochón Por Fuckin Dios!"

Handkerchiefing sweet smelling horse and Marlboro boy sperm from everywhichwhere, including the killum stack, we dropped our sticky hankies on the floor for the overpaid Berber janitor to deal with.

Grunting, rearranging our clothes – so satisfying – I wondered what Mustapha would do after he was humiliated and blackmailed? Return to his Long Beach State Physical Education Department Ohhh! as a fuck instructor? Or did they need one there?

Hushed awe, "Oh my Mustapha master, you're the best real man I ever had, with good personality and so sensitive too!" The whole damned redwood leaned against me; it was neat having power over such a hulk.

"But I want all, all of you in me!" kneeling, kissing his spermy monster fist, frenching its hairy back. Hah! He was fucking loco if he thought that cannonball would ever go up my previously-looted but still-intact treasure chest!

Confused Saliva confession time, sucking on his hairy dick finger (not *that* one!), "But – but Mustapha – I've never gone, all, all the way before!"

Horse moans, pushing my head to his rising limb again. Enough! I pulled my head back to talk, "So you'll have to work on it first, like last time, oh I was so loose and

168

relaxed! And if you really wanna drive me wild, yell at me real loud about all your previous hot fucks with Tangerino men and their wives, what you did and what they did to you, okay, Mustapha honey?"

Hobbyhorse shaking, wild forelegs grab-throwing me up into his waterfalling Mt. Rushmore for Assholes horseface, sucking my distinguished nose discharging madly, "Oh, my sweetest Frisco slutbitch! I remember how you make me feel and everything I do to you! I replay it, in my mind, every lonely night. But tonight I show you why mighty Mustapha was most popular foreign student at Club Baths on Melrose in Hollywood, oh, my Club Baths Ohhhh!"

My little Marlboro boy's face drowning in horse tears; Berber strawboss had dismissed self and lug crew for afternoon lunch, siesta and prayers for two or three hours. Get me outta here, goddesses, my aged joggers pedalling on his jellaba'ed tree trunks as he held me aloft, his sobbing liver-sized tongue washing my mouth.

"I, I must-must," freeing my dainty mouth. "Oh, Mustapha, we must return upstairs now, you wanted to talk to desperate and distracted Ms. Dawson about all those worthless old killums she won't be able to get rid of."

Mustapha set me down, nice but bossy horsey, "You wait me here, outside, 10 p.m. tonight, for real L.A.- Frisco game!" I guess we wouldn't have to load the camera.

Giant's sigh, "But your Joe Montana the best. I like get him in my Club Baths, and that Jerry Rice — I like the skinny ones too, and Blacks real nice to me there."

One last fisting my squirming Levi's for the stairs, "Oh Mustapha, you're too much! I can't wait! Maybe I'll ask a friend if I can borrow his sling for tonight, you know, like at the baths back in the fun Crisco Disco '70's."

Horse blowing nostalgically, fisting me scrambling up the stairs, "I thought I'd hang it from the light grid up above our little love table."

169

Mastadon death grip on stairs, "No, you dumb Frisco faggot, lights fall down on us with my wild Mustapha fuck action. We hang your sling from strong wood transformer box in middle, I do it for you. I know everything here, I and my brother install everything for Mr. Dawson when he was boss here."

Stab in the dark, "Oh yes, I heard about your lucky brother running off with Mr. Dawson to Nueva York."

Shaking cheeky Califas Pussboy on the stairs, huge horse teeth bared, "In America we have old saying, Never Speak Bad of Dead One!"

My teeth, everything clacking, "Oh, so sa-sorry La-Long Ba-Bitch Ma-Master, ta-night!"

Not wanting to prespoil his merchandise, Mustapha set me down, opened the upstairs door, free! Except for his dominant whinnying, "Don't forget 10 o'clock outside, I bring screwy-eyes, Frisco sling twat get full tonight, run over!"

I skittered off to lunch, siesta, and prayers for the rest of the day, to prepare for cocky Joan's whippin' Bette's bitchy ass, after we took our painpleasure por diosas!

Making two harnesses hadn't been much more work than making one, though the Clydesdale one took twice as many wide leather strips as the spritely colt sling. The big horse's sling was covered with jingle bells, while the little one had velcro Krazy-glued to it, burr side out.

We did it all at disapproving Abdullah's, including Apache strategy pow-wows, for I didn't trust my friendly Berber granny to keep her nose away from my bluestriped killum door. As she did, I think(?) when Sweet Ali arrived from Fes and we spent every spare moment for a couple of days in total immersion Spanglish in my blue killumed bed.

Faithful pony Ali had taken a short vacation from his

English studies at Fes U. to come up and help his object of worship. "I help you everything forever against puto Tangerinos!" still pissed about his wallet stolen in the market here. "And you help me when we live on Mission District, mi amigón amorazón mi fucking corazón!" Sweet Ali's Spanglish was muy romántico.

Ali and Khalid squabbled of course as we sat measuring, cutting and sewing our leather slings in Abdullah's cell. The kerosene lantern above the head of the bed was lit for Abdullah's reading escapist French sex novels and our sling preparation.

It was tiresome sitting on the floor in our sewing circle between the antagonists, ordering Ali in English and Khalid in Spanish to shutfuckup their Arabic bickering. Which language to use with whom got confusing, especially as the kif wore on, so I'd end up in Spanglish which Abdullah understood best.

But he wasn't listening. He said my self-indulgent First World vengence was misplaced, that I should be swinging George and that sexy blond pussyboy Dan in dollar-covered slings from the White House chandeliers, instead of misdirecting my maniacal energies on a pathetic misfit like Mustapha.

But I knew they'd never let me take my slings into the White House, and how would we overpower the Secret Service, much less Barbara? "Brighten the Corner Where You Are," I sang the old hymn to him; he got the metaphor.

Laughing again, Abdullah pushed me back to my sling work, and his long sex fingers back to the object of his dirty French novel. At least it was gay, he assured me, with just enough bi thrown in to keep it interesting. I threatened to tell his father the shit I was driving him to read, but sensible pirate son wouldn't give me his phone number.

I taught my squabbling sewing squaws the harmonies

of Sunday morning Protestant singing, our conflicting accents making it more beautiful:

Brighten the corner where you are
Brighten the corner where you are
Mustapha far from Heaven jingle-slinging oh so far
Brighten the corner where you are!

Repeat chorus, repeatedly.

HONEST KHALID DOES HIS JOB

Four silent Apache Pierres in daypacks slipped single-file through the dark Medina, destination, Dawson y Dawson Exports, objective, Operation Hobbyhorse at last! Of course adventuresome Abdullah was along; we both knew he would be in spite of his sarcastic belittling of my "camelbrained jihad scheme."

A couple of blocks from Op HH, the three Marhueco Apaches melted away. Earlier reconnaissance had revealed the camera was loaded and ready, entry gained by resourceful Berber brave gloming onto an extra doorkey when harried Liz was only half-watching him.

Shiny black jellaba'ed hobby Clydesdale was rocking the lighted doorway. Excited tree-hug hello, then he opened the door with his key; was that why we were going bankrupt?

Rushing down to the basement, Mustapha stood on a modest stack of killums on goldblack inspection bench to secure one large screwy-eye in the center of the wooden box up in the lights; I resisted cautioning him not to hurt the camera. My crafted white velcroed, black leather sling on a silver chain made goofy horse nicker with envy. I promised to lend it to him so he could have a larger model made. Even if he didn't swing in it, hanging it on his bedroom wall would impress and turn on tricks, we agreed.

Grateful horse tongue enveloping my face, foreplay kicking in, clothes kicked off, inspection begun under the floodlights to The Doors' Greatest Hits, perfect taste, Mustapha! But he had too much horse sense to shout out his Tangerino bisexual history as I'd requested, for it was *his* camera up there we were playing to, he thought.

Kneeling horseface was slurping pink Saliva treasure chest twitching crazily in velcroed black leather sling when stealthy Abdullah thrust a hypodermic needle into

173

Mustapha's vast plantation ass. He bellowed, turned and collapsed on the table with a mighty thud for a perfect camera shot through my best wide-eyed, hand-clapped-over-mouth Joan C. horror in a sling!

Efficient Apache technicians fitted the horse into his hand- and leg-cuffs, then shout-struggled me into mine. I resisted macholy for the camera, of course. Nude fuzzy drowsy Clydesdale into his red leather sling covered with jingle bells, another screw-eye on bottom of the box (we'd weight-tested it), and the horse sling hauled up on its gold chain.

Another injection and horse awoke bulging-eyed, screaming expletives in Engabic in his jingling sling, swinging against me, screaming terrified and sobbing in my own velcro film project at last!

The three Apache terrorists leaped up on the blackgold torture table, their ski masks covered with flattened Marlboro cartons, red and white. In purple warm-up suits, with no crotches.

They doubled and redoubled their fists with their hardongs sticking straight up — for the camera. They surrounded Horsey and me on his humiliation/revenge film set. I didn't wanna do anything too elaborately Hollywood or Mustapha would have known for sure I was the brains behind his ass rape.

Mock terrified swinging: "Oh Mustapha! What's happening to us? Are these your friends? Oh save me, my Allah boy!"

But enraged nude Spartacus was too busy to talk, thrashing wildly on his back, hand- and leg-cuffed, massive zep bouncing. The three confused sex terrorists tried to contain him, jingle bells clanging, The Doors pounding. Our wackiest home video was going perfectly — if crazed Clydesdale Spartacus didn't wreck the set, crashing the ceiling down on us.

I screamed convincingly until the Marlboro-masked

terrorists in purple warm-up suits let me down roughly. Arabic cursing, they slapped and kicked naked hand- and leg-cuffed me. For my cover, of course, but they were acting a bit too sincerely, I thought, even Sweet Ali!

Abdullah shot up bellowing Spartacus again with horse tranquilizer, then waved his needle and hardong threateningly at me. I was cursing them in Spanglishabic and spitting on their stupid Marlboro masks.

Then a slam at the top of the dark basement stairs. Didn't those stoned nitwits remember to lock the door? Or did everyone in Tanger have a key? Was that why we were going –

I didn't see who was shooting automatic fire down on us as I fell off the torture table and ripped off my fake cuffs.

The gunfire stopped, except in my ears, when an ululating scream erupted from the dark at the top of the stairs. I'd know that scream anywhere. Sueád? Not a nurse, not an L.A. karate instructor – but, a what? Too bad we all had to get killed to find out. But I hadn't even seen a camel here yet! Well, maybe now I'd become one – a move up or down the reincarnation scale?

Boots on the stairs, guttural Spanish shouts: "Those bullets are in the wall, but the next ones will be in you if you don't all get back up on that table. Now!"

The pathetic sex terrorists and one of their victims complied. Their other hostage was silent in his swing. He knew what bullets meant.

I stood beside and clutched my three fellow pieces of dead meat. Oh no, I'd fantasized this all ending differently: outraged but bewildered flaming-asshole Mustapha blackmailed and humiliated; Abdullah tricking poor Khalid with an invalid visa, left sobbing and vowing revenge at the Tanger airport. And Sueád, our helpful but disapproving Paris body guard. And me super-pissed, not speaking to my perfect lovelust, asshole Abdullah, sitting next to me

175

on First Class Air France to Paris, sipping his champagne and chuckling cynically at *Le Monde*, with silent serious Sueád in Khalid's seat across the aisle.

But instead, here we were, five bobbing faggots in the shooting gallery. Oh, my poor parents, they'd have a real Baptist test when their queer youngest son's bullet-riddled body got shipped home to Kansas in an African box.

No time for fantasizing, must listen to the low Spanish voice, obviously fake, now coming from the dim at the bottom of the stairs: "Don't let me interrupt your fun, gentlemen. Go right ahead with your little party. Lights, camera, action!"

Sueád had seen too many B Hollywood movies, dubbed into Arabic(?) French(?) Spanish(?) These people spoke too many languages.

We trembled, I whimpered, standing on the front edge of the table, our mighty hardongs wilted, worried about performance.

Again the rough voice from the dim: "Take care of that worthless piece of business hanging there like his mother's saggy twat!"

Horsey snapped to life, muttering Arabic curses and fighting his restraints. Emboldened by fear, we surrounded our sacrifice, praying his execution would relax God's trigger finger. Or our Goddess'.

Deciding this was a good time for Love, I took the lead and plunged my tongue into Horsey's protesting mouth that groaned and sucked me in. But Horsey howled and nearly bit my tongue off; I jerked out and looked up. My three fellow victims were standing at the foot of the beast, between his hairy legs spread wide. Arms around each other, they laughed and thrusted. Were they all plowing poor Mustapha at the same time? I mean he was big, but not – . Oh well, it would help prepare him for the fist fucking. My god, they had six of those!

Cum groans I recognized came from the three

resurrected sex terrorists. My, they were easily distracted from an Uzi. They withdrew and knelt before their horse's holy cave, and I swear, horny Abdullah's head disappeared completely! Well, best get Horsey loosened up before they stuck god only knew what up there. The Uzi too?

Oh, our captor — I'd almost forgotten. A glance told me she was still in the shadows across the room. She must have seen me look at her: "You there, white boy! Get your hungry ass back up there in your sling for a little workout!"

Oh no, that wasn't the plan! I'd never even been four-fingered before (well, maybe when I was real drunk or stoned), much less fist fucked with an Uzi waving at me. That could be rape; not to mention murder.

But Uzi knew best, so, shaking, I numbly fumbled back into my little sling, blurring. What would my parents think about my proud Baptist asshole all tore up? Well, maybe that drunk fool undertaker, old Calvin Perwinkle, would have the decency to spare them the grisly details. But he was so normal, a scandalous gossiper, that everyone would soon know I died with my friends' fists ravaging my bunghole.

Gruff: "You, the tall one! I want to see you up to your armpit in the Americano whore there!"

Shivering, I stood up in my harness. I saw blood dripping on the blackgold killum on the other end of the inspection table. The wounded horse moaned, but his tormentors had taken a break. All eyes were on Abdullah as he stepped to the edge of the table to address the dim force. Some horse blood was splattered on him and his noble cock was softening, slick and pointing down through his crotchless purple warmup suit.

Quiet anger: "Come on, Sueád, I know it's you. I'm truly sorry about your demotion. I argued against it. But my father pays, so it's his way."

Gleeful low anger: "Wrong again, pretty boy. I am connected with a certain person who asked me to come

177

here tonight, to represent certain of her, or his, interests. I am told that your typical rashness and irresponsibility caused you to open your door to that dope dealer, really a drunken assassin from Mustapha's family. So one day a certain person is your head body guard, the highest woman in the family, and the next, working on one of your father's drug-smuggling boats — as a cook!"

Abdullah hung his Marlboro head. "Look at me!" snapped the dim. "That's the last humiliation your dirty-hands father will play on me, I mean on her, or him. They taught me to shoot. Now they'll see how well."

Sprouting from around his Marlboro mask, Abdullah's springy curls slowly shook "No."

Jim Morrison lighting her fire, Sueád glided forward silently into the edge of the light from the inspection table. She was dressed as a man in dark pants, boots, jacket and hat, Uzi erect. But she was too far away for us to jump her. Oh well, as the Greeks said, all politics are local. So I'd just politely go along and let the locals handle this one. So glad I could think rationally at a time like this, but I still couldn't feel myself. I noticed my hands were concealing, and hanging onto for dear life, my depleted privates.

Sotto snarl from the semi-dim: "Stop shaking those cutesy ringlets of yours, Miss Abdullah. They make you look like the sissy nymphomaniac dope addict you are. Waving your ugly thing in my face when we were kids, and the dirty things you bullied me into doing. That was no way to treat your first cousin! And I hope the baby looks exactly like you. Your father will receive a plentitude of baby pics."

I gasped. First cousins? Knocked-up? Just like Kansas!

Brave Abdullah had not stopped shaking his Marlboro curls: "You know you'll never get away with this, Sueád. If you're determined to pursue your persistent death wish — how many times is it now? — I'd recommend that you

178

do it to yourself, and spare the innocent by-standers."

"Innocent?! You? And that thieving puto Khalid? Two less Por Dios pieces of Tangerino street trash. And the decadent blondie Americano there? Ha, he looks better in the nude than he sounds. When I listened to the tapes from our bug in Abdullah's room, blondie squealed like a satan pig. Señora Susana would barge in and make me explain what you all were doing during your 'Pierres.' She's going to take some of the most disgusting tapes with her to the Rif Mountains. To enliven her retirement, she says."

Abdullah low, lightly insistent: "You won't get out of this alive, Sueád, unless you leave right now. Go to Paris, get a new life."

Snappy: "Exactly what I intend. Then the bank in Switzerland, and by the time they find your rotting corpses down here, I'll be god-knows-where on one of my false passports. But I'll make copies of your fuck death video tape and spread them around. Your families will be so proud of you."

Abdullah's slow head shaking: "You kill an American and you'll have all those bloody fascists chasing after you."

Her Uzi swung towards me. "Ha! They probably can't stand him at the Embassy either!" (Not true; I'd never been there.)

Lecturing me in low español: "You're so loud and rude. And so vain with your smartass 'Spanglish.' You reek of psuedo-cultural superiority. And bringing your decadent diseases here, corrupting our local boys. Well, not those two," indicating Abdullah and Khalid with her Uzi.

Harsh chuckle: "But you were funny up on the terrazza of the safe house when you hit your neck on the clothes-line. And I had to 'save' you. Worse than an old Kansaño woman!"

My body jerked. At least I was feeling insults. And the alleged safe house? There wasn't a safe house in this burg.

Uzi swung to Abdullah: "Okay, you haul the Americano up and sex and violence him. The camera is rolling and we don't want to bore our audience. They'll call this part, 'Decadent Revenge against Capitalist Imperialism.' Come on, string him up."

Abdullah spread his hands, "Sueád, you know I can't do that."

Oh, noble Abdullah! Better death than hurt his heart, his true love. He continued, "I can't let my father see me doing that weird shit."

Oh, best to strangle love before its words choke you! A matter of self-defense. Which jolted our minds as Sueád squeezed off a burst of automatic Uzi babies too close to ducking Abdullah.

He smartly stepped beside me and grasped the silver chain to haul me up.

I whispered, "Take it easy, Big Boy, okay? I still love you, even though you did impregnate our killer, you immoral slut, you!"

Adullah growled behind his Marlboro mask and jerked the chain. I was sprawling in the air again, belly up.

Muttering in Arabic, I hoped it was complimentary, Abdullah pushed my legs apart and moved in for the kill. My tight Baptist asshole was conveniently located at fist level. He picked up a tube of Vaseline (Product du Maroc) from the table at his feet and greased his right arm to his elbow.

Hemorrhage flooded my brain; I'd always thought I'd die a clean death, falling off a mountain cliff somewhere. Not tortured bleeding to death, and maybe shot, too!

A long finger squeezed in my ex-treasure chest, its lock, its jewels forever shattered. It whispered, "Relax," as pain jabbed my ass, in the cheek not facing Sueád.

Oh, clever Abdullah had grabbed the horse tranquilizer hypo along with the vaseline. A greater numbness was

180

spreading back there. I hoped he hadn't OD'ed me. Like it mattered at this point. At least I'd die unconscious.

"Thanks for the drink, and everything else, Perfect Abdullah," I whispered, sensing a stretching back there and feeling the presense of hugeness moving in and up.

Drunken, I heard slurred words I had trouble connecting: "And you, Ali. Move slowly and get down off there. Get out of that ridiculous Las Vegas clown outfit and change back into your street clothes in your daypack. Do it in front of me, here."

Ali obeyed, carefully retrieving his pack from under the table.

"Go directly to the train station and take the midnight train back to Fes. You are salvagable. Return to your university and study science instead of English so you can help our people, instead of selling yourself to the foreigners like a she-whore."

Hardening: "I'm sparing your life, Ali, don't make me regret it. If you ever breathe a word about here, tonight, your whole shit-eating family will have their throats slit."

Sueád returned her attention to our Imperialist Revenge tableau. Sweet Ali leaped behind her, slashing at her throat. With a handy shafra from his pack? Funny, I mused, screaming there while this freight train chugged up my tunnel. It all happened in seconds but in slow motion for me.

Wild Uzi oozings, huge Horsey red-running limp in his jingle-belling sling, twirling around, bullets from struggling Sueád piercing his tough hide.

A shining camel rose from his sling, smiling in perfect golden cameldom. Eternal Lovelust at last, Jim Morrison's voice leading him into the white light to home, "Salaam-alíacomb, Hámdullah!"

The train pulled out of my station which collapsed with a sucking sound. Abdullah fell off the back of the table. But faithful Khalid, diving for dirham, hurled himself into

181

me, fumbling at my chain. No, it was Love, his job. I'd always known; he'd been with us before and would be again.

I floated to the table as bullets knocked my savior down. I rolled on top of Khalid and tore off his Marlboro mask. He giggle whimpered sweet lies, "Thank you, gracias mi amor. You were everything to me."

I tasted warm salty liquid and greedily swallowed Honest Khalid's last blood. Silence, sweet peace, The Doors done and Suead finally dead by Ali's knife.

Abdullah and Ali barked sharp Arabic, their hands pulling me off my dead brother and roughing me into my clothes. They dragged me up the stairs without a look back at the carnage wrought by my little joke gone too far. I didn't feel anything, but I would, I would, I would.

The night was quiet, between my two surviving boy friends to Sueád's old Renault parked on the street. Abdullah unlocked it (did everyone have a key?) and pushed Ali and me in. He spoke rapid-fire instructions to Ali in Arabic and pushed some bills into his hand as we reached the lights of the train station.

Ali, crying, got out and started to kiss me goodbye but drew back when he saw Khalid's blood still on my lips. I treasured it; I'd never wash again. He embraced me through the car window and walked alone towards the train station.

Abdullah put the car in gear and drove off calmly. "Ali will return to Fes. Don't worry about him, I'll see that my father takes care of him financially so he can finish school and study whatever the fuck he wants to. And no one will know what he did – down there."

I watched the black streets blur by. Weakly, "But, but what about the video tape? We're all on it!"

Stopped at a traffic light, Abdullah leaned over and kissed me on the lips. He didn't mind Khalid's blood. "Don't worry, locochón, I'll call my father from the airport

182

and he'll clean up the mess. What are fathers for?"

Shock and horse tranquilizer waning, blubbering began: "Oh, and poor Khalid, it's—it's all my fault! And Mustapha and Sueád too!"

Abdullah clasped my hand as he drove. "Well, locochón, it was your bright idea, but I'd say it was more my fault. I should have known better than involve you in our little family dispute."

I jerked my hand away. "Huh? You mean you and Mustapha are family?"

He retook my hand — he was stronger than me and I couldn't resist. "No, you know, Sueád and I are, were, kissing cousins. Mustapha's family is sometimes our opponent and sometimes our ally in, uh, business."

I squeezed his hand, trying to hurt him. He chuckled. So I cried harder, "Oh poor Khalid, he died protecting me, and we just left him there!"

Abdullah smiled as we entered the Medina's maze of narrow streets. "My father will give him a proper wailing funeral and burial. Let's face it, with his crazy fucking life, it was just a matter of time till he was dead, or in jail, or both. Same goes for Mustapha. And Sueád."

"But your ba–baby — dead too!"

"Just another of Sueád's pathetic lies, locochón. You know I'm always faithful to you."

I shot him a dirty look, but this was no time for a fight. He stopped the car on the street above his room. "We'll clean up and get your stuff, and some downers for our pains." (It was starting to burn down there, but that was a small price to pay.) "Then the night flight to Paris where we'll decide what's next. Maybe I should give the States a try. You got any good schools over there?"

I grinned through my tears, "You mean the Saliva Christian College, home of the Horny Bible Thumpers? Maybe they'll cure you of sticking your fist up innocent Kansas boys."

183

Abdullah pushed me, ruffled my hair and laughed. "I thought that was the part you liked best. As for schools, I was thinking of something more like U.C. Berkeley. I hear it's locochón-city there."

We climbed out of the car and held each other on the dark Tangerino street, deserted except for a floating trio of golden camel ghosts, laugh-harmonizing Saliva Baptist hymns in classical Arabic, brightening the corner perfectly, for us.

THE END

OTHER GLB FICTION

The Bunny Book US $11.95 ____
Novel by **John D'Hondt**

A Classic of literature that deals with AIDS...
                                    – Robert Glück

Snapshots For A Serial Killer US $10.95 ____
Fiction and Play by **Robert Peters**

Beautiful, layered, taut, weird, surprising...
                                    – Dennis Cooper

Zapped: Two Novellas US $11.95 ____
Two Novellas by **Robert Peters**

Comic book gestalt, as featured in *Atom Mind*.

The Devil In Men's Dreams US $11.95 ____
Short Stories by **Tom Scott**

Sentiments from ironic humor to painful remorse...
                                    – Lambda Book Report

White Sambo US $12.95 ____
Novel in stories by **Robert Burdette Sweet**

Powerful and touching vision of gay life...
                                    – Shelby Steele

ADD $2.00 PER BOOK FOR SHIPPING/HANDLING (US) ____

Check or money order to: **TOTAL**
____
G⏥L⏥B Publishers
P.O. Box 78212, San Francisco, CA 94107